Acclaim for Eric Ambler and

STATE OF SIEGE

Eric Ambler

STATE OF SIEGE

Eric Ambler was born in London in 1909. Before turning to writing full-time, he worked at an engineering firm and wrote copy for an advertising agency. His first novel was published in 1936. During the course of his career, Ambler was awarded two Gold Daggers, a Silver Dagger, and a Diamond Dagger from the Crime Writers Association of Great Britain, named a Grand Master by the Mystery Writers Association of America, and made an Officer of the Order of the British Empire by Queen Elizabeth. In addition to his novels, Ambler wrote a number of screenplays, including *A Night to Remember* and *The Cruel Sea*, which won him an Oscar nomination. Eric Ambler died in 1998.

ALSO BY ERIC AMBLER

STATE OF SIEGE

Eric Ambler

STATE
OF SIEGE

VINTAGE CRIME/BLACK LIZARD

Vintage Books

A Division of Random House, Inc.

New York

The Library of Congress has cataloged the Knopf edition as follows:
Ambler, Eric, 1909–
[The night comers]
State of siege / Eric Ambler.
Originally published: The night comers. London :
William Heinemann, Ltd.
p. cm.
I. Title.
PZ3.A48 St
55005610

Vintage ISBN: 0-375-72677-2

www.vintagebooks.com

Printed in the United States of America
10 9 8 7 6 5 4 3 2 1

STATE OF SIEGE

1

The weekly Dakota from Selampang had never been known to arrive at the valley airstrip before noon, or to leave on the return journey before one. After the farewell party they had given for me the previous night, I should have slept until eleven at least. But no; I was wide awake, packed and ready to go at dawn.

Not that I had had much packing to do. Most of my clothes—the *dobi*-battered slacks and bush shirts, the mosquito boots and the sweat-stained hats—I had given, with my camp bed, to Kusumo, who had been my servant for the past three years. The few things that were left—shoes, some white shirts, underwear and other personal oddments—had gone easily into one small metal suitcase. The only suit that I possessed, I wore. Like a fool, I had ordered it by mail from an outfitters in Singapore, and it hung on me like a shower curtain; but that morning I did not care how I looked; nor, indeed, how long I had to wait for the plane. What mattered most to me just then was the fact that I was leaving, and that in my breast pocket, along with my passport and a ticket for a B.O.A.C. Qantas flight from Djakarta to London, was a letter. It was from the Singapore branch of the Hongkong and Shanghai Bank, and advised me that, on the completion of my contract as resident consulting engineer to the North Sunda Power and Irrigation Project, there stood to my credit the sum of fifty-eight thousand eight hundred and ninety-six Straits dollars.

Soon after eleven, I borrowed one of the maintenance department jeeps and drove across to the Chief Engineer's office to say goodbye.

Now that I was leaving the place I could look at it with friendlier eyes. As the jeep bounced along the corduroy road past the new *attap* houses and the row of quonset huts in which the European employees lived, I was even aware of a feeling of pride in what had been done.

It was a Colombo Plan project, and there had been no shortage of American and British Commonwealth capital to finance it; but it takes more than money and good intentions to build dams in places like the Tangga Valley. When I had first arrived at the site with the advance party, there had been nothing but swamps, jungle, leeches and a colony of twenty-foot pythons. It had taken the contractors nearly a month to get their first two bulldozers up from the coast; and there had been a period during the first year, just after the monsoon broke, when we had had to abandon all the equipment and move up to the high ground in order to stay alive. Yet now there was a camp as big as a small town on the site, and an airstrip, and, there, wedged in the throat of the valley, the huge mass of stone and steel and concrete that was the keystone of the whole project. Because of that dam, it had been possible to turn something like two hundred square miles of scrub country down by the Tangga delta into rich padi fields. That year, for the first time, Sunda would have surplus rice to sell to the neighbouring islands of Indonesia; and when the power station below the dam was completed and the transmission lines began to reach into the tin- and tungsten-bearing areas to the north, there was no telling how prosperous the young state might not become. The Tangga Valley scheme was something to be proud of. My own motives for going to Sunda had been in no sense noble or disinterested. I had been paid as much for working for three years in the Tangga Valley as I would have been paid for working for ten years, and tax free, in England. But there had been satisfaction in the job for its own sake, too. I might be sick to death of Sunda and delighted to be leaving it, but I had come to like the Sundanese and was glad that I had been of service to them.

There were two other men already in the Chief Engineer's office when I put my head round the door, but Gedge beckoned me in.

"Sit down, Steve. Won't keep you a moment." He turned and went on with what he had been saying. "Now, Major Suparto, let's get this straight . . ."

I sat down and listened.

Gedge, the man in charge of the job for the contractors, was a South African civil engineer of great ability and experience who had spent most of his working life in the East. Moreover, he had done so from choice. He had worked for many years in China and, since the Japanese war, in India and Pakistan. There, he had made no secret of the fact that he preferred Asians to men of his own race, not merely as working associates but also as friends. Among the Europeans, he had, not unnaturally, a reputation for eccentricity, and from time to time inaccurate rumours that he had Communist sympathies, or six Eurasian concubines, or that he had secretly become a Buddhist, would find their way across the bridge tables.

At the moment, however, his feelings towards his Asian collaborators were anything but friendly. He was having trouble with them. Indeed, since Major Suparto and his five brother officers had arrived from Selampang six months earlier, there had been practically nothing but trouble.

❀

Sunda used to be part of the Netherlands East Indies. In 1942 it was occupied by the Japanese. When the Dutch returned three years later, they were confronted by a Sundanese "Army of Liberation" and a demand for independence which they were unable in the end to resist. In 1949 Sunda became a Republic.

The moment of greatest difficulty for all revolutionary leaders seems to be the moment of success; the moment when, from being rebels in conflict with authority, they themselves have suddenly become the authority, and the fighting men who procured the victory wait jealously, and inconveniently, for their reward. Armies of liberation are more easy to recruit than they are to disarm and disband.

At first, it looked as if the Provisional Government of the new Republic of Sunda were dealing shrewdly with this embarrassment. A policy of dispersal was applied to break down *esprit de corps.* No unit was disbanded as a unit. Men who came from the same district were collected together and then transported back to that district, before being disarmed and demobilised. Meanwhile, the Government rapidly built up the small regular army on which their authority was to rest in the future, and used it against any of their former supporters who showed fight. And, of course, some did; particularly the younger soldiers, who frequently banded themselves together and terrorised the people in the villages. But this sort of brigandage had little

7

political importance. For some months after the proclamation of independence by President Nasjah all
seemed to be going fairly well.

Unfortunately there was an aspect of the problem
that the Government had neglected. In their anxiety to
dispose of the rank and file, they had not troubled to do
anything about disposing of the officers; and by the
time they had realised the gravity of that mistake, it was
too late to retrieve it.

There were several hundreds of these surplus officers; many more than could conceivably be absorbed
by the regular army or by the new police force. Moreover, many were not officers in the ordinary sense of
the term, men sensitive in matters of loyalty, but guer-
rilla leaders and ex-bandits who had both fought and
collaborated with the Japanese occupation forces before
doing those same things with the Dutch colonial
troops, and who might reasonably be expected to start
fighting the new Government in Selampang if the
promised Utopia did not immediately materialise; or if
they became dissatisfied with their share of the spoils.
With such men, making revolutions may easily become
a habit. Machiavelli thought that the wise usurper
should, as soon as he comes to power, trump up charges
against his more ambitious supporters and have them
killed off before they can get into mischief. But not all
politicians are so wary or so practical.

Even when the danger had become manifest, the

Nasjah Government underestimated it. Struggling with vital day-to-day problems of administration and caught up in the political battle being waged over the new Constitution, they felt that they had no time to spare just then to deal with petty discontents. No doubt something would have to be done soon, but not now. With the peculiar innocence of politicians in office, they even assumed that as long as the surplus officers continued to draw their pay and allowances they would remain loyal to the leaders of the Republic. Had these men not fought to make it all possible? Were they not, after all, patriots?

The politicians soon had their answer. By the time they were ready to submit the Draft Constitution to the General Assembly, there was an insurgent force of nearly three thousand men operating in the central highlands. It was led by an ex-colonel named Sanusi, who promoted himself to General and rapidly gained administrative control of an area which straddled the only two roads connecting the capital with the northern provinces. Moreover, Sanusi was a devout Moslem and issued a series of manifestos calling upon all True Believers to join his Sundanese National Freedom Party and declare a Holy War on the infidels in Selampang who had betrayed the new state at the very moment of its birth.

The riots which ensued caused some casualties among the Eurasian population of the capital, but order

9

was eventually restored without much bloodshed. Although most Sundanese are Moslems and a majority of the men wear the black cap of Islam, religion is not an important factor in their lives. It was General Sanusi's hold on the interior of the country which constituted the real problem. A punitive expedition sent against him had to withdraw ignominiously when one of its regimental commanders deserted, together with all his men and most of the expedition's ammunition supply. A subsequent series of air attacks on what was believed to be Sanusi's headquarters resulted, because of the hazardous flying conditions in the mountains, in the loss of two out of the ten obsolete planes that constituted the Government air force.

Having swallowed these humiliations, the Government were forced to examine the problem more realistically. They believed that Sanusi possessed neither tanks nor artillery, and that without them he would be obliged to remain in the hills. They knew, too, that any further loss of face on their own part would shake the public's confidence badly. Foreign sensibilities had also to be considered. Arrangements were almost completed for large United States dollar credits to be placed at their disposal. An appearance of calmness and stability must be preserved at all costs.

So they decided to bluff.

A communiqué issued by the Minister of Public Enlightenment announced that the "Sanusi gang" had been rounded up and liquidated, and a directive to newspaper editors ordered them to refrain from all further allusions to the "incident." Political murders committed by Sanusi's undercover agents in Selampang were to be blamed on "colonialist reactionaries." For inquisitive foreigners who wanted to know why it was still impossible to travel by road from the capital to the north, there was a bland statement that, in view of the extensive damage to bridges and mining of roads carried out by the retreating Dutch forces during the war, land communications would take at least a year to restore. Meanwhile, both sea and air transport were readily available.

At the same time, the Minister of Defence was instructed to take special and secret precautions against any further treachery in the armed forces. The reliability of every army officer was to be carefully tested by the use of *agents provocateurs*. A list of the dissident was to be compiled and steps taken to render them harmless. Sanusi was to be left to cool his heels in the mountains until a full-scale offensive could be mounted against him.

The feeling of security which the Government derived from the making of these decisions did not last long. The inquiries made by the Minister of Defence soon provided the frightening information that there was open talk of a *coup d'état* among the officers, that a group was already in secret communication with Sanusi, and that it was doubtful if more than a third of the officers of the Selampang garrison could be relied upon in an emergency.

The Council of Ministers' first reaction was to panic, and for an hour or so, apparently, there was wild talk of asking for a British warship from Singapore to stand by. Then, they pulled themselves together and gave General Ishak, the Minister of Defence, special powers to deal with the conspirators. Within twenty-four hours, sixteen senior officers had been shot and a further sixty were in prison awaiting court-martial.

The immediate crisis was over; but the Government had been badly frightened and they did not forget the experience. The news from Indonesia of the "Turko" Westerling incident intensified their anxiety. If a small force of Javanese counter-revolutionaries led by a few mad Dutchmen could capture a city like Bandung under the very noses of the lawful Indonesian Government, a large force of Sundanese insurgents under Sanusi could probably capture Selampang. Only the Selampang garrison, with its Japanese tanks and armoured cars and its six German eighty-eights, prevented their trying. If Sanusi could ever neutralise the garrison by allying himself with a Fifth Column conspiracy of the kind that had so nearly succeeded before, the game would be up. From now on there must be extreme vigilance. Reliable police spies must be found to report on the activities of all officers and former officers. The

malcontents must be dealt with shrewdly. With a determined trouble-maker, a knife in the back would be
the only safe solution. With a more self-interested man,
however, a well-paid civil appointment might be the
best answer. If, besides purchasing his loyalty, you
could also expect to gain his services as an informer, an
even more lucrative post could be awarded.

As self-interest seemed to be the dominating charac-
teristic of most of the officers on the list of suspects,
the new policy worked. From time to time there were
plot scares and midnight executions, and for one period
of a month martial law was declared; but although the
roads to the north were now permanently in insurgent
hands (Sanusi impudently collected taxes from the
villages in his area), the Government did not lose any
more ground. The losses they suffered from now on
were in terms of morale rather than territory.

The black market, for example. There were simple
economic reasons for its growth. The American credits
had been spent not on capital goods, but dissipated on
such things as cars, refrigerators, radios and air-condi-
tioning equipment, the importation of which had produced huge personal commissions for members of the
Government and their subordinates. Efforts to control
the resulting inflation had been half-hearted. "Inducement taxes" had been imposed only to be evaded. In
Selampang there was a black market in practically
everything. In the tuberculosis clinics set up by the

World Health Organisation, a *mantri* would even in-
ject water into his patients so that he could steal the
B.C.G. vaccine and sell it on the black market. All
kinds of racketeering flourished. In Asia, admittedly,
the giving and taking of bribes is a normal, accepted
part of the daily business of getting things done; but in
Sunda it assumed stultifying proportions.

Yet, the Government, although recognising the need
for measures to deal with the problem, were quite unable to agree what those measures should be. It was not
mere indecision, and it was not simply because there
were some ministers with personal interests to consider.
Their inability to deal effectively with this or any of the
other social and economic problems which confronted
them had a deeper cause. The Sanusi affair had in some
subtle way served to demoralise them completely. Certainly, after the discovery of the conspiracy of 1950, the
whole business of government in Sunda was conducted
in a deadly atmosphere of guilt, greed and mutual suspicion that made any major decision seem horribly
dangerous. The Nasjah Government, in fact, was suffering from a recurrent nightmare, and their fear of it
incapacitated them. A watertight plan for eliminating
Sanusi was the only thing that could have produced
unanimity.

Up in the Tangga Valley we were to some extent
isolated from all this madness; at least during the first
year. We used to be told about what was going on by

14

visitors, especially World Health Organisation and UNICEF people who came to work in our area, and be surprised that such intelligent men should expect us to believe the fantastic stories they told. Later on, when our own contact with the capital became closer, we knew better. But as long as Gedge had the labour force he needed and supplies continued to come up to us from our small port on the coast, we were able to feel that what went on in Selampang was no concern of ours.

And then the "government nominees" began to arrive.

It is one of the basic principles of Colombo Plan policy that, when aid is given for a project like the Tangga River dam, as many of the managerial posts as possible should be held by Asians. If qualified Asians are not immediately available and Europeans (i.e., whites) have to be employed under contract, then every effort has to be made to replace them with Asians when those contracts expire. Obviously, this is good sense, and, naturally, a man like Gedge was in eager sympathy with the principle. But the operative word is "qualified." Asia is desperately short of technicians of all grades, and at the managerial level the shortage is acute. In Sunda, the position was as bad as could be.

However, that fact did not deter the authorities in Selampang. When a government depends for its physical safety on a policy of "jobs for the boys," highly paid jobs become scarce. Furthermore, the salaries were paid by the Colombo Plan contractors, not by the Government. When the Europeans' service contracts began to expire, the Tangga Valley project must have looked like a gold mine in Selampang. Innocently, Gedge assumed that his formal, routine requests for Asians to replace the departing Europeans (requests that he was legally obliged to make) would be acknowledged and then forgotten in the usual way. He knew perfectly well that they had nobody suitable to send him. And he was right.

The first surplus officer to report for duty was a brutish-looking man in the uniform of a captain of infantry, who announced that he was taking up the post of surveyor to the project and then demanded a year's salary in advance. On being questioned as to his qualifications, he stated that he was a graduate of the new School of Economic Administration at Selampang, and produced a certificate to that effect. He also produced a pistol which he fingered suggestively during the remainder of the interview. I was there and it was a nerve-racking hour. In the end Gedge gave him a warm letter of recommendation for a post on the central purchasing commission (whose salaries were paid by the Government) and held the plane so that the captain could return at once to the capital and present the letter.

The captain soon proved to be a fairly typical example of what we had to expect. After three other would-be surveyors had been returned, together with a dozen or more candidates for other jobs, the Ministry of Public Works had changed its tactics. Instead of sending the applicant in person, it would send his name, together with an imposing account of his alleged qualifications, certified as correct by the Minister of Public Works. This left Gedge with the choice of accepting the applicant unseen at the Ministry's valuation, or of questioning the valuation, and thus, by inference, the Minister's honesty.

In the end, both sides had to compromise. The Ministry promised to stop sending half-witted gangsters who had been found unemployable even by Sundanese standards. Gedge agreed to take on six Sundanese officers with experience of administrative duties as "liaison managers." The real jobs were filled, as Gedge had always intended they should be, partly by re-engagement, partly by promotion and partly by bringing in new men, Asian and European, from outside.

I think that we all thought that he had made a good bargain. Friendly relations with the Government had been preserved. His own authority had been unimpaired. His employers' interests had been safeguarded. The work could now go forward smoothly to its completion (as per specification and on schedule) and to the moment when he would stand bare-headed in the breeze above the eastern spillway accepting the President's congratulations. Permission had arrived from the contractors' head office to debit the salaries of six use-less Sundanese officers to the contingency account. All that remained now was to see if the Government kept faith with him.

In their own tortuous way they did keep faith. They did not send half-witted gangsters. They sent intelligent ones.

They arrived all together, four majors and two captains, by special plane from the capital, and began by complaining that the Chief Engineer was not there to welcome them officially. They then announced that they would wait until he arrived. I was with Gedge when he got the message.

He sighed. "I see. Prima donnas. They mustn't get away with that. Would you mind going over, Steve?"

"Me?" Strictly speaking, it was no concern of mine. Labour relations were the contractors' business. I was there to represent the firm of consulting engineers who had planned the project, and to see that the contractors did the work according to our specifications. But I had always got on well with Gedge and could see that he was genuinely concerned.

"If someone senior doesn't go they'll lose face," he explained; "and you know I can't afford to start off badly with these people."

"All right. But it'll cost you a couple of large Scotches."

"Done. And if you go right away I'll make it three."

I was not to know that he was, in a way, saving my life.

I found the new arrivals standing in the shade by the radio shack, glowering into space. The jeep drivers who had been sent to collect them looked terrified. I got out of my jeep and walked over.

They were all very smartly turned out, their uniform shirts spotless and their pistol holsters gleaming. I was a bit impressed.

As I approached, they turned and stiffened up. One of the majors took a pace forward and nodded curtly. He was a slim, handsome little man with the flat features and high cheekbones of the southern Sundanese, and a tight, arrogant mouth. His English was almost perfect.

"Mr. Gedge?"

"No. My name's Fraser. I'm the resident consulting engineer. You are . . . ?"

"Major Suparto. I am glad to meet you, Mr. Fraser." We shook hands and he turned to the group behind him. "I introduce Majors Idrus, Djaja and Tukang, Captains Kerani and Emas." There were more curt nods as he turned to me again.

"We had expected Mr. Gedge to give us the honour of welcoming us on our arrival, Mr. Fraser."

"You are certainly welcome, Major. Unfortunately, Mr. Gedge is rather busy just now, but he would like to see you gentlemen in his office."

Major Suparto appeared to consider this. Then, suddenly, he smiled. It was such a charming, good-humoured smile that it deceived me for a moment; as it was meant to. I nearly smiled back.

"Very well, Mr. Fraser. We will accept you as Mr. Gedge's deputy." The smile went as suddenly as it had arrived. "You do not think that if we went to his office immediately he would be busy merely in order to keep us waiting?"

"We haven't much time here for protocol, Major," I said; "but you will have no reason to complain of discourtesy."

"I hope not." He smiled again. "Very well. Then we can go. Perhaps I may drive with you, Mr. Fraser."

"Certainly."

The rest followed in the other jeeps. As we went, I explained the geography of the camp, and stopped at a point on the track from which they could all get a view of the dam. There were exclamations of wonder from the jeeps behind us, but Major Suparto did not seem greatly interested. As I drove on, however, I saw him examining me out of the corners of his eyes. Then he spoke.

"What is a liaison manager, Mr. Fraser?"

"I think it's a new appointment."

"And unnecessary, no doubt. No, do not answer. I will not embarrass you."

"You're not embarrassing me, Major. I just don't happen to know the answer to your question."

"I admire your discretion, Mr. Fraser."

I took no notice of that one.

"I am a reasonable man, Mr. Fraser," he went on after a bit. "I shall be able to accept this situation philosophically. But my companions are a little different. They may look for other satisfactions. Things may grow difficult. I think that it would be as well for Mr. Gedge to remember that."

"I'll tell him what you say, but I think you'll find that he'll be very understanding."

He did not speak again until we pulled up outside Gedge's office; but as I went to get out, he put a hand on my arm.

"Understanding is a fine thing," he said; "but sometimes it is better to carry a revolver."

I looked at him carefully. "If I were you, Major, I wouldn't make any jokes like that in front of Mr. Gedge. He might think that you were trying to intimidate him, and he wouldn't care for that."

He stared at me, and, although his hands did not move, I was for a moment acutely aware of the pistol at his belt. Then, he smiled. "I like you, Mr. Fraser," he said; "I am sure that we shall be friends."

The meeting with Gedge passed off fairly well. All the liaison managers claimed to have had administrative experience. A more surprising thing was that they all spoke some English. Although English is now a second official language in Sunda (Malay being the first) not many Sundanese can speak it yet. There was some tension when the discrepancies between what they had been told about their jobs in Selampang and what they were told by Gedge became apparent, but, in the end, they seemed to accept the situation good-humouredly enough. Major Suparto nodded and smiled like a father pleased with the behaviour of his children in adult company. Later that evening, there was a further meeting with heads of departments. They had all been warned in advance and were ready. Each one had to take a liaison manager. In effect he would be a kind of trainee. Let him potter around. If he could make himself useful, so much the better. If not, it would not matter.

None of them claimed any technical knowledge. Major Suparto asked to go to transport. The supply, plant, electrical, construction and power-lines departments took the rest.

The first hint of trouble came three days later from the construction department. Captain Emas had attacked and badly beaten up one of the men working in number-three bay of the power house. Questioned about the incident, Captain Emas stated that the man had been insufficiently respectful. The following week two more men were beaten up by Captain Emas for the same reason. The truth emerged gradually. It appeared that Captain Emas was organising a construction workers' union, and that the men who had been beaten up had shown a disrespectful reluctance to pay dues. The secretary and treasurer of the union was Captain Emas.

Gedge was in a difficult position. All the project labour had been recruited locally and such minor disputes as had arisen had hitherto been settled by consultation with the village headmen. No formal union organisation had been found necessary. Unfortunately, under the Sundanese labour charter, membership of a union was obligatory for manual workers. Captain Emas obviously knew that. If he were fired and sent back to Selampang, he would simply complain to the Ministry of Public Works that he had found an illegal situation and been victimised for trying to remedy it. The Ministry would be delighted. In no time at all, Captain Emas would be back armed with special powers to organise all Tangga Valley labour.

Gedge chose the lesser evil. He called a meeting of headmen, reminded them of the law, and secured their agreement to his applying to the labourers' union in the capital for an official organiser. He also instructed them that a record of all dues paid to Captain Emas must be kept in future so that Captain Emas could be held accountable for them later. He then called Captain Emas in and repeated the instruction in his presence.

That took care of Captain Emas for a few weeks, but it soon transpired that Majors Djaja and Tukang had been operating the same racket in the plant and electrical departments. Further meetings of headmen proved necessary.

All this was tiresome enough. The headmen felt that their authority was being undermined and were being obstructive; the workmen resented having to pay union dues just because somebody in Selampang said they had to, and were slacking on the job; small difficulties were beginning to cause big delays. But there was worse to come.

About fifteen miles east of the valley camp, on the road up from Port Kail which was used by the supply trucks, there were several big rubber estates. Two of these were still run by Dutchmen.

The position of the Dutch who remained in Sunda was both difficult and dangerous. The majority were employees of the few Dutch business houses which, under Government supervision, were still permitted to operate; banks, for example. The rest were mostly rubber planters in out-lying areas where anti-Dutch feeling had been less violent; men who, rather than face the bitter prospect of having to abandon everything they possessed and start afresh in another country, were prepared to accept the new dangers of life in Sunda.

For the Dutch, those dangers were very real. When there was trouble in the streets, the greatest risk that any European ran was in being taken for a Dutchman. After a ghastly series of incidents in Selampang, the Chief of Police had even made a regulation authorising any European in charge of a car involved in an accident to drive right on for a kilometre before stopping to report to the police. If he stopped at the scene of the accident, both he and his passengers were invariably beaten up, and often murdered by the crowd. Men or women, it made no difference. The explanation that the victims had seemed to be Dutch would always serve to excuse the crime. Dutch owners of rubber estates were in an almost hopeless position. They were not allowed to sell or mortgage their estates, except to the Government, who would pay them in blocked currency which could not be exported. If they continued to operate their estates they had to sell their entire output to the Government at a price fixed by the Government. On the other hand, they had to pay their estate workers at minimum wage rates which made it virtually impossible for the estate to remain solvent. If they wanted to survive, their only chance was to conceal a proportion of their output from the Government inspectors and sell it for Straits dollars to the Chinese junk masters who made a rich business out of buying "black" rubber in Sunda and running it to Singapore.

Mulder and Smit were both men of about fifty, who had spent most of their lives in Sunda. Mulder had been born there. Neither had any capital in Holland. Every guilder they had was in their estates. Moreover, both had Sundanese wives and large families of whom they were very fond. Inevitably, they had decided to stay.

In the early days at the camp we had seen a good deal of both men. During the first few months, indeed, before the road was properly completed, we had used their guest rooms almost as if we rented them. Smit was a huge, red-faced man with a fat chuckle and an incredible capacity for bottled beer. Mulder had a passion for German *lieder,* which he would sing, accompanied by a phonograph, on the smallest pretext. With each other they played chess; with us, poker. Later, we had been able to repay some of their hospitality, but they never really liked coming to the camp. No women were allowed in the European club, so we could not ask them to bring their wives; and there were many Sundanese in the camp for whom the mere presence of a Dutchman was an irritant. When the liaison managers arrived I had seen neither of them for weeks.

Early one morning about three months before I was due to leave, Mulder drove into the camp with the news that Smit and his wife had been murdered.

The first part of the story was easily told. At one o'clock that morning, Mulder and his wife had been wakened by the Smits' eldest son, a boy of sixteen. He said that two men had driven up to the bungalow half an hour earlier and battered on the door until they were admitted. The noise had wakened him. He had heard his father speaking to them and there had been an argument. His father had become angry. Suddenly, there had been four shots. His mother had screamed and more shots had been fired. The men had then driven away. His mother and father were wounded. He had left the ayah to look after them and run for help.

By the time Mulder had arrived at the bungalow, Smit was dead. The wife had died shortly afterwards. Later, he had taken the children and their ayah back with him to his bungalow. Fearing for the safety of his own family, he had stayed with them until daylight before driving up to the camp to ask us to report the matter by radio to the police at Port Kail.

From the way he told it, it was fairly obvious that he knew more than he was saying. When I got him alone and had promised to keep my mouth shut, he told me the rest.

A week earlier two Sundanese had come to see him with a proposal. They said that they knew that he was smuggling rubber out of the country and being paid for it in Straits dollars. They wanted a half share in the proceeds of all future consignments. If they did not get it, unpleasant things would happen both to his family and to him. They would give him two days to think it over. Meanwhile, he was to tell nobody.

He went to Smit and found that the men had been to see him also. The two planters discussed the situation carefully. They knew that they were helpless. There was, of course, no question of their appealing for police protection. Apart from the fact that they would have to admit to the smuggling, which for Dutchmen would be suicidal, there was also the possibility that the men themselves might be connected with the police. They decided, in the end, to pay up, but to bargain first. They thought that an offer of ten per cent might satisfy the men.

It did not. The men became angry. They gave Mulder a further twenty-four hours to agree, and also demanded two thousand Straits dollars in cash as an earnest of his intentions.

That had been the previous night. The men must have gone straight to Smit, realised from what he said that the victims had been consulting together, and decided to show Mulder that they meant business. They had succeeded. Mulder was ready now to give them his whole estate if they asked for it.

But I was still a bit puzzled. Smit had not been the sort of man who is easily intimidated. It was difficult to think of his opening the door to a couple of thugs in the middle of the night without a loaded gun in his hand. As for Mulder; if he had asked me to help him to ambush the two men and leave their bodies for the kites, I should not have been greatly surprised.

It was not until I had persuaded him to talk about the two men that I understood. It would have been death to touch either of them. They were Sundanese army officers, a major and a captain. The descriptions that he gave left me in no doubt as to their identity. I persuaded Mulder to go with me to Gedge and repeat the story.

That night when Major Idrus and Captain Kerani arrived at Mulder's bungalow, Gedge and I were waiting behind the screen doors into the bedroom. We heard them describe what they had done to Smit and his wife, and threaten Mulder with the same treatment if he did not pay. Then we came out armed with shotguns and a shorthand record of what we had heard. For a while the air was thick with protestations. In the end, however, a deal was made. If Major Idrus and Captain Kerani left Mulder alone, we would take no further action. Mulder would lodge our signed statements at his bank, so that if anything happened to him the statements would go to the police. It was a miserable arrangement, but, short of involving Mulder in police inquiries, it was the best that we could do. Idrus and Kerani were smiling when they left to drive back to the camp in a supply-department truck. They had reason to smile; they had got away with murder.

We stayed behind with Mulder for a while and drank too much gin. For Gedge it did not improve the occasion.

"How would you like to stay on here, Steve?" he asked suddenly as I drove the jeep back to the camp.

"What do you mean?"

"You can have my job if you like."

"No, thanks."

"Wise man. It's not going to be pleasant having murderers about the place."

"Understanding is a fine thing," I said; "but sometimes it is better to carry a revolver."

"What's that?"

"Something that Major Suparto said."

And now I was sitting in Gedge's office for the last time, listening to what was being said, yet knowing that in less than three hours what I was hearing would seem as remote as a dream.

Unlike his five brother officers, Suparto had been an unqualified success. The ability to plan and organise is rare among the Sundanese; but, in this respect, Suparto was exceptional by any standards. Secure in a two-year contract, the Transport Manager had no qualms at all about delegating authority to so able and energetic an assistant, and had resisted the efforts of other departmental managers to lure him away.

Suparto had outlined the situation crisply.

There had been a strike of stevedores down at Port Kail the previous week and some important machinery had been unloaded on to the quayside by the ship's crew. Now, the Customs people were making difficulties about identifying the individual items on the ship's cargo manifest, and were refusing to clear it. In his opinion they were turning a small confusion into a big one in the hope of getting a substantial bribe. He believed that if he were to go down to Kail and see the head of the Customs himself, the problem would very soon disappear. The Transport Manager shared that belief.

"We've never had trouble with the Customs before," Gedge was saying; "even in the early days when they could have made things good and tough for us."

"Major Suparto thinks that the local men may be getting squeezed from above," the Transport Manager said.

"I think it is possible," said Suparto; "but that is not something which can be discovered by radio telephone. I must talk with these men privately."

Gedge nodded. "Very well, Major. We'll leave it to you. The main thing is to get that machinery on its way up here. How long will you be away?"

"Two days, perhaps three. I propose to leave at once." He turned to me. "Mr. Fraser, I shall not have another opportunity. May I wish you a safe journey and a happy future?"

"Thanks, Major. It's been a pleasure knowing you."

We shook hands and he went out with the Transport Manager. Then began the rather more elaborate business of saying goodbye to Gedge.

The Dakota arrived at twelve thirty. When they had off-loaded the two mailbags, some cartons of dried milk and a couple of small air-compressor sets, they put my suitcase aboard and slung the outgoing mail in after it. My successor and one or two particular friends had come out to the airstrip to see me off, so there was more nonsense to be talked and handshaking to be done before I could get aboard myself.

Roy Jebb was the pilot. The first officer was a Sundanese named Abdul. They never carried a full crew on those trips, so, as I was the only passenger, I sat in the radio operator's seat just behind them. The plane had been standing in the sun for an hour and was suffocatingly hot inside; but I was so glad to be going that I did not even think to take my jacket off. I could see the men who had been seeing me off walking back to where the jeeps were standing, and wondered vaguely if I would ever see any of them again. Then the sweat began to trickle into my eyes and Jebb called to me to fasten my seat belt.

Two minutes later we were airborne.

2

The dark green mass of the jungle moved away beneath us and we began to follow the coast line with its ragged fringe of islands and turquoise-coloured shoal water.

Jebb glanced over his shoulder at me. He was lean, rangy and very Australian.

"Done anything about getting yourself a room, Steve?" he asked.

"I thought of trying the Orient."

"You might get a bed there. You won't get a room to yourself. Isn't that right, Abdul?"

"Oh yes. You can't sleep alone in Selampang. That is what they say." The first officer giggled deprecatingly. "It is a joke."

"And not a very funny one. They've got six beds now in some of those fly-blown rooms at the Orient. It's a fair cow."

"I'll buy my way in," I said; "I have before. Anyway, it's only for three days. I'm hoping to get a plane to Djakarta on Friday."

"You can try if you like, but you'll still have to share with a stranger. Why don't you come over to the Air House with me?"

"I didn't know they let rooms."

"They don't. I've got a little apartment up top there over the radio station. You can doss in the sitting room if you like."

"It's kind of you, but . . ."

"No 'buts' about it. You'd be doing me a favour. I've got to go to Makassar tomorrow and won't be back till Friday. It's asking for trouble these days to leave an apartment unoccupied."

"Thieves?"

"Either that or you come back and find some bloody policeman's wangled a requisition order and moved in with his family. I lost my bungalow that way when I went on leave last year. Now, I always try and get a pal to stay, even if it's only a couple of days."

"Then, I'll be glad to."

"It's a deal. What do you want to do on your first night of freedom?"

"Where's the best food now?"

"The restaurants are all pretty bloody. Did you know we've got a new club? The New Harmony it's called."

"It's a year since I've been down here."

"Then that's settled. Your evening's made. Now then, Abdul, what about some tea? Where's that thermos?"

Selampang lies at the head of a deep bay looking westward across the Java Sea. It used to be called Nieu Willemstad, and along the canals near the port there are still a few of the old houses, with brown-tiled roofs and diamond-paned windows, built by the early Dutch colonists. It stands on what was once swamp land, and the network of canals which covers the whole city area is really a system of drainage ditches; ditches in which the majority of the inhabitants, serenely ignoring the new sanitary regulations, continue to deposit their excreta, wash their bodies, and launder their clothes. When the Dutch left it, Selampang had a population of of about half a million. Now it has over a million and a half. Yet, when you drive along the wide, tree-lined streets of the modern sections, past the big solid bungalows standing in their spacious compounds, there are no signs of overcrowding. It is only the pervasive smell of the canals and the occasional glimpses you get of the teeming *attap* villages which encrust their banks that remind you. The new slum city has grown like a fungus behind the colonial façade of the old.

The Air House was on the south side of the big Van Riebeeck Square, next to an eighteenth-century Residency which housed a department of the Ministry of

Public Health. The highest and the newest building in Selampang, it had been put up by a consortium of oil companies and airline operators as an office block, and was nearing completion when the Japanese occupied the city in 1942. For a time the Japanese had used it as a military headquarters; then their psychological warfare people had moved in, erected lattice masts on the roof and made a short-wave radio station of it. After the war it had remained a radio station. Only the ground floor had been handed back to the airline operators, and this was now a booking office and the terminal for the airport bus.

Jebb's apartment was on the top floor. The lift only went to the fifth; after that you walked along a rubber-floored corridor, through some swing doors and up a flight of stairs. Beyond the doors the building was still unfinished. The concrete of the auxiliary staircase was as the builders had left it in 1942. Footsteps echoed dismally down the staircase well. The window openings were roughly boarded up and it was not easy to see where you were going.

"Mind yourself here. You'll catch your coat," Jebb said.

We rounded a concrete upright bristling with the ends of reinforcement rods and walked a short way along a dusty passage. Then Jebb stopped at a door and took a key out.

"They'd just started to put the drains in these apartments when the Japs came," he said. "This is the only one they finished. The other five are still empty. After all this time and with a housing shortage, too! What a country! I had to bribe the whole of the city hall before I could even get the water turned on."

He opened the door and we went in.

My spirits had been drooping a little as we mounted the stairs, and I was remembering the camp bed I had so confidently given away; but inside things were different. There was a small tiled hall with a kitchen leading off it and another door into the sitting room. This was long and narrow, but almost the whole of the outer wall was taken up by french windows leading on to a deep terrace with a concrete balustrade. Over the terrace there was a plaited bamboo sun roof and, at the sides, *attap* screens. There was not much furniture; apart from the usual bamboo long chairs and a divan that was clearly used as the spare bed, there was a radio, a portable phonograph, a bookcase full of paper-backed novels and a bamboo serving trolley with drinks on it. On the walls were some Balinese pictures. It was cool and comfortable. I said so.

"The girl-friend helped me fix it up." He started the ceiling fan going very slowly. "Got to watch this bastard. Don't switch it on too quickly or it'll blow the main fuses down on the floor below. Now, what's it to be, Steve? Drink first or shower first? I'll tell you what. We'll have a long drink first while I show you where everything is. Then we'll shower and go on from there. What'll it be? Brandy dry? Gin fizz? Scotch if you like, but if you want to stay on the same thing all the evening, brandy or gin are easier. I'll go and get the ice."

When he had made the drinks, he showed me his bedroom and then took me out on to the terrace. It faced north, and from one end you could see out over the funnels and masts of the shipping in the port and across the bay. Beyond one of the *attap* screens at the other end was a Dutch bathhouse with a big stone ewer of water and a galvanised iron scoop.

"What do you know about it?" he demanded. "My word! Fancy putting a thing like that in a new building."

"Some people say it's the best sort of shower there is."

"Not me. Sloshing the water all over yourself with a thing like a saucepan, when you could pipe it up another four feet to a sprinkler—it's crazy! Besides, you have to be a bloody contortionist to rinse the soap off all over. The can's okay though—ordinary civilised type. Last place I had, it was practically the old pole-over-the-pit."

"How long have you been here, Roy?"

"In this country? Four years. Don't get me wrong. There's a lot I like about it besides the fat salary they pay me. But they're a funny lot. For instance, all these things they're getting now, like cars and fridges and radios, they don't look on them just as things to use. They *wear* them like lucky charms. Doesn't matter if the thing's any use to them or not, or even if it works. They've got to have it to feel all right. Abdul saw an American wearing a gold wrist-watch in a movie, so *he* had to have a gold wrist-watch. He starved himself for three months to pay for it. Why? He never looks at the time, he doesn't wind the bloody thing, he's not even particularly proud of it. It's just *his.* They're mostly like that, and that's what fools you. You think they're simply a lot of show-off kids trying to ape western civilisation."

"Until one day you find out that they're not simple at all, and that you haven't ever begun to understand them."

"Too right. You know, when I was new here, I once asked a bunch of them at the airport what they thought was the most serious crime a man could commit. Know what they said?"

"Not murder anyway. They think we're too fussy about that."

"No, not murder. To steal another man's wife, that was the worst, they thought."

"I've never heard that one before."

"Neither had I. I didn't know then that it's no use asking questions in this country. You only get the answer they think you want to hear. During the war my

wife went off with another man. I'd just divorced her.
Those jokers happened to have found out, that's all."
He grinned. "You married, Steve?"

"Not any more. Same story."

He nodded. "Mina'll fix you up all right."

"Who's she?"

"The girl-friend. Tell you what. You have the
shower first. I'll go and call her up now and tell her to
bring a friend along."

It was dark when we went down into the square
again and the whole place had come to life. There were
people everywhere. The casuarina trees and travellers'
palms which ringed the gardens in the centre were fes-
tooned with lights, and market stalls had been set up
beneath them. Chinese food-sellers surrounded by little
groups of eaters squatted in the dust. A boy of about
ten sat on his haunches playing a bamboo xylophone,
while another beside him beat a drum. The road which
ran round the square was jammed with crawling cars,
and the *betjak* drivers rang their bells incessantly as
they manoeuvred their brightly painted tricycles
through the gaps. It was a tribute to the wealth and
influence of the Selampang black-market operators
that, in a city where the cheapest American car cost
three times as much as it cost in Detroit, there should
be a modern traffic problem.

There was a line of empty *betjak* by the Air House
entrance and, as soon as he saw Jebb, one of the drivers

swung out of the line and pedalled up to us, smiling eagerly.

"We need two this evening, Mahmud."

"I can take both, *tuan*."

"Maybe you can, sport, but we want to be comfortable. Where's your friend?"

Another driver was summoned and we set off.

Once you have learned to disregard the laboured breathing of the driver pedalling behind you and have overcome the feeling that you are the sitting target for every approaching car, the *betjak* is an agreeable form of transport, especially on a hot night. You are carried along just fast enough for the air to seem cool, but not so fast that the sweat chills on your body. You can lean back comfortably and look up at the trees and the stars without being bitten by insects; and, providing the driver does not insist on muttering obscene invitations to the nearest brothel in your ear, you can think.

I was glad of the respite. After the Tangga hills Selampang was suffocatingly humid, and even a light cotton shirt seemed like a blanket. Also, I had had three large brandies at the apartment; one more than I really wanted. I would be busy the following day and had no intention of burdening myself with a hangover. I had no intention either, I told myself, of spending the night with some local drab selected by Jebb's girl-friend. I had heard his telephoned instructions, and decided that there was a point at which hospitality became officiousness. Besides, the breaking of a habit of continence, especially if it has been enforced, should not be too casually enjoyed. I had my own ideas about the occasion, and they did not, at that moment, include Selampang.

The New Harmony Club was outside the city. Beyond the race track there was a stretch of about a mile of straight, unlighted road, with large bungalow compounds on either side of it. It was very quiet on this road, and you could hear an approaching car almost as soon as you saw its lights. Even the cicadas seemed muted, and we had left behind the smell of the canals.

"Nice part this," Jebb said; "as long as you're not too near the race track." The two *betjak* were travelling abreast now.

"Who lives here?"

"Foreign legations mostly. One or two rich Chinese. They have to pay through the nose for the privilege though. Look, there's the club. That light ahead. Shove it along, Mahmud! We need a drink."

It was a bungalow much like the rest, but with an electric sign by the entrance to the compound, and a gatekeeper in a peaked cap who peered at us intently as we turned in. As we stopped, the warm, humid air seemed to close in again, but now it was heavily scented by the frangipani growing in the forecourt; and from inside came the lush, sentimental, international sound of a night-club pianist playing American music.

In the vestibule a Chinese doorman in a sharkskin dinner jacket made out a temporary membership card for me, and sold me a pack of American cigarettes at double the black-market price. Then, we went through into the room beyond.

Once it had been two rooms, but arched openings had been cut in the old dividing wall to make it one. There was a teak-panelled bar at one end and a platform with the piano on it in an alcove. The rest of the space inside was filled with tables, about a dozen of them. Out on the covered terrace there were a few more tables and a small raised dance floor. The walls were painted to imitate stonework, and the light came from electric candles in wrought-iron wall brackets.

It was early, and only two or three of the tables were so far occupied. The bar, however, was crowded. Most of the men were Europeans, though there were a couple of slick young Sundanese in air-force uniforms sitting on bar stools and a neat Chinese with rimless glasses. The pianist was a supercilious-looking Indian wearing a gold bracelet and a ruby ring. A Dutch couple were leaning on the piano with glasses in their hands, listening to him raptly. The wife's hair was untidy and she seemed to be a little drunk. The Indian was ignoring them.

"'A bunch of the boys were whooping it up in the Malamute saloon,'" Jebb quoted facetiously, and began to elbow his way towards the bar, exchanging greetings with people as he went. "Hullo, Ted. How're you doing, sport? Hi, Marie."

Marie was a stout, dark girl with big, protruding teeth and a tight silk dress. She smiled mechanically and blew cigarette smoke at the ceiling. Jebb winked at me. I had no idea what the wink meant, but I grinned back understandingly. The effort was wasted. He was greeting the Chinese with the rimless glasses.

"Evening, Mor Sai. Want you to meet a pal of mine, Steve Fraser. Steve, this is Lim Mor Sai. He owns the joint."

As we shook hands, a middle-aged blonde with haggard eyes and a foolish mouth came through the door beside the bar and slipped an arm through Jebb's. "Hullo, Roy love," she said. "I thought you were going to Makassar."

"No, that's tomorrow. Molly, this is Steve Fraser. Steve, this is Molly Lim."

She gave me a glassy stare. "Another bloody Britisher, eh? Why don't you people stay at home?"

I smiled.

"One day, my darling," said her husband primly, "you will make such a joke too often. Then, a lot of our furniture will be broken and there will be trouble with the police."

"Oh, go on with you!" She fondled his cheek. "He knows I'm pulling his leg. I'll give you three guesses

44

where I come from, Mr. Fraser, and the first two don't count."

"Lancashire?"

"Of course. Mor Sai says I even speak Cantonese with a Liverpool accent. Isn't that right, love?"

Lim looked bored with her. "As this is your first visit to the club," he said to me, "you must have a drink on the house."

"That's what we've been waiting to hear," said Jebb. "We're drinking brandy."

"You'll find it on the bill," said Mrs. Lim sardonically and moved away.

Lim snapped his fingers for the barman and gave the order. Jebb nudged me. I glanced across the room and saw Mrs. Lim snatch a glass out of a man's hand and swallow the drink at a gulp. The man laughed.

Lim saw it, too. The moment our drinks came, he excused himself and went over to where she was standing.

"I ought to have warned you about our Molly," Jebb said. "Don't buy her a drink, whatever you do."

"It doesn't look as if she waits to be bought one."

"Yes, you have to hold on to your glass when she's around. That bastard should know better. He'll be unpopular with Lim if he's not careful."

"Is that a bad thing?"

"It's as well to keep on the right side of him. Lim's

got friends in the police department. You know the time they take over exit papers? A week sometimes if they feel bloody-minded. Last time I went on leave, Lim got everything for me in a couple of hours, and I bet you . . ." At that moment he broke off, grinned over my shoulder and said: "Hi, Mina baby!"

I looked round.

Eurasian women are difficult to describe accurately. One's first impression is always dominated by one set of racial characteristics to the virtual exclusion of the other; but closer acquaintance always seems to reverse that first impression. It is not just a matter of clothes; a European dress can make the same woman look both more Asian and less; the change is as unpredictable as it is with those optical illusions with which you may make a pyramid of solid cubes become a pyramid of empty boxes, merely by blinking.

At first sight Mina looked completely European. She was a slim, attractive brunette with the sort of aquiline bone structure that you find mostly in the Eastern Mediterranean; Greek, you might have guessed. Her friend, Rosalie, on the other hand, looked like a Filipino girl of good family who had learned to wear her clothes at an American university. Yet, after ten minutes, Mina's features had become for me unmistakably Sundanese, while Rosalie looked like a European girl who was modelling her appearance on that of her favourite ballerina. Their voices had something to do with it. Both spoke good English with Dutch accents; but in Mina's voice you could hear the Sundanese gutturals as well. She was tense and emphatic. Rosalie was quieter and more self-assured.

Jebb had explained that they both taught Western dancing at a school run by a Chinese, and that we would be expected to pay them for spending the evening with us at the club. After midnight, further negotiations would become necessary; but I would have to conduct those myself. With Mina, he had a more or less permanent arrangement. Rosalie was known to be very choosey; if she did not like you, there was nothing doing, even if you were a millionaire. It was up to me.

I was resigned, then, to a dull and probably squalid evening. It turned out to be neither. I think that the thing which broke the ice for me was the realisation that, unsentimental though it might be, the relationship between Mina and Jebb had at the same time a basis of genuine affection. I don't think I was being ingenuous. You can be deceived about loving, but not so easily about liking.

Mina talked a great deal at first. Most of the time she was playing a favourite Sundanese game. If you owe a man money, or if he has caused you to lose face in any way, or if he is someone in authority whom you dislike, you invent a scandal about him, preferably with a wealth of scatological detail, suggesting that he is impotent, cuckolded or perverse. Nobody believes the story, but the more circumstantial you make it, and the more carefully your audience listens, the more superior to your enemy do you become. Mina's scandals were pungent and outrageous and she told them like a good comedienne, with a sort of bland amazement at their strangeness. Jebb's part was to refuse to believe a word she said. If, for example, the story was about the Chief of Police, Jebb would declare that he knew the man personally and that her story was impossible. This in turn would lead to a further extravaganza in order to prove the first.

It could have been boring, but for some reason it wasn't. Once or twice, when I laughed outright, she would laugh too, and then hasten to persuade me that what she had said was no laughing matter. Rosalie only smiled. Her attitude towards Mina was that of an adult towards a precocious child who may become over-excited; amused but guarded. Now and again I saw her out of the corner of my eye watching me shrewdly and weighing me up. I was surprised to discover that I did not mind. Once, she realised that I was examining her. She was saying something to Jebb at the time, and the realisation made her hesitate for a word; but otherwise she seemed completely self-possessed.

The dinner was Vietnamese and very good. After it we moved out on to the terrace and drank tea. Then, Lim switched on a record-player and we danced for a while; but the small floor soon became too crowded for comfort and we wandered out into the compound.

Once there had been a garden neatly laid out with stone walks and flower beds and ornamental fish pools; now, it was all overgrown, the crotons and banana trees had run wild, and the pools were choked with Java weed. But the air was pleasantly scented and I was glad to get away from the noise of the record-player. I lit a cigarette and for a minute or so we walked along a path that had been roughly cleared to one side of the compound. Then a bat fluttered close to my head and I swore. The moon was very bright and I saw the girl look up at me.

"You do not have to be polite to me," she said.

"What do you mean?"

"It is eleven o'clock. Mina and Roy will not leave for two hours yet. You have had a long journey today. I think you must be very tired."

"I've enjoyed this evening, but now, yes, I am tired."

"Then you should go and sleep." She smiled as I hesitated. "We can meet again tomorrow if you wish."

"Yes, I'd like to do that. Roy's going to Makassar tomorrow morning and I know no one else in this place. No one, that is, that I want to see." I hesitated again. We had stopped and she was looking up at me.

"What is it you wish to say?"

"There is my side of the bargain too."

"I do not think we need to talk about that. You will be here for two, three days. When you leave you will give me a present of money. If we have not liked each other, you will give it in contempt. If we have liked each other, it will make the parting easier. In any case you will be generous."

"Are you sure about that?"

"Yes, I am sure."

That was all that was said. She took my arm and, in silence, we continued the circuit of the compound. It was a fine night and I suddenly felt peaceful.

We were walking along the path that ran parallel to the lane beyond the boundary fence, when I saw a light flickering through the bamboo thicket ahead of us.

"What's that light?" I asked.

"There are some old kampong houses there. When the Dutch people were in the bungalow, that is where the servants lived. But I did not think that they were used now."

The stone surface of the path had ended and we were walking on soft earth that deadened the sound of our footsteps. Then we heard voices ahead, and our pace became slower. One of the voices was Mrs. Lim's and neither of us, I think, wanted to encounter her just at that moment. I was about to suggest that we turn back, when she began to shout at the top of her voice.

"And I say they can't! Do you want us all murdered? You're out of your bloody mind!"

A man said something quickly. Mrs. Lim uttered a sort of gasp, as if she had been hit, and then began to weep.

Rosalie's hand tightened on my arm. Suddenly, there was a faint clatter of feet on wooden steps and then the sound of someone, Mrs. Lim presumably, hurrying back towards the bungalow.

For a moment we stood there uncertainly. We had half turned to go back; but the shortest way back to the bungalow was straight ahead, and there seemed no point now in retracing our footsteps. We walked on.

The servants' houses were among some palm trees on the far side of a rough track that led from a gateway on to the lane. It was wide enough for a bullock cart and had probably been used as a sort of tradesmen's entrance. The houses were built on teak piles, and the frames were substantial enough, but the *attap* walls had suffered in the monsoons and both places looked derelict. The light, which looked as if it came from a kerosene vapour lamp, was in the house farthest away from the track, and it shone through the tattered walls. A low murmur of men's voices came from within. There seemed to be four of them. By the steps up to the verandah of the nearer house stood a jeep.

Jeeps are common enough in that part of the world. It was a bracket welded on to the side that made me stop and look at it. Quite a number of the ex-army jeeps had that bracket; it had been fitted originally to support a vertical exhaust pipe when the jeep was water-proofed for driving out of a landing-craft; but this one was bent in a vaguely familiar way. I glanced down at the number.

In a place where you depend on mechanical transport for practically every move you make, even a highly standardised vehicle like a jeep acquires character, has its own subtle peculiarities, its special feel. You prefer some to others, and because they all look the same you learn to differentiate between them by their numbers.

I knew the number of this one only too well. I had already seen it once that day. It had been standing outside Gedge's office.

I must have made a startled movement, for Rosalie looked up at me quickly.

"What is it? What's the matter?"

"Wait here a moment."

The house with the light was about twenty yards away. I walked towards it. At that moment my intention was to go in and ask what the hell a jeep from the Tangga Valley project was doing down in Selampang. Luckily, by the time I had covered half the distance, I had come to my senses and stopped. It had been about eleven a.m. when I had last seen the jeep in Tangga, and yet here it was just over twelve hours later in Selampang. It could not have come by sea in that time. It could not have come by air. That meant that it had been driven down two hundred miles by road. Which meant, in turn, that it had been passed quickly and safely through every road block manned by the insurgents in Sanusi's area, as well as the outposts manned by the Selampang garrison. That meant that the person who had been in it was someone to stay well away from at that moment; and that applied to his friends, too.

I stood there for a second or two with my heart thumping very unpleasantly. I could distinguish the voices inside now. They were speaking Malay. One man was repeating something emphatically. His voice was light and ugly and sounded as if he were trying to speak and swallow at the same time.

"All of them. We must have all," he was saying.

The voice that replied was certainly Major Suparto's. It was very calm and controlled. "Then it must be de-layed until the second day," he said. "There must be patience, General."

I turned quietly and went back to Rosalie. She said nothing and took my arm again as we walked back towards the club.

When we had gone a little way she said: "Is there something wrong?"

I hesitated. I thought she might think that I was being stupid. "That jeep back there," I said at last. "It was in Tangga this morning. A Sundanese army officer drove it here today—by road. A major. He's in there now."

53

I need not have worried. The implication, when she saw it, made her draw in her breath.

"With Lim Mor Sai?" she said quickly.

"I suppose so. There were others there, one of them a general. I think we'd better forget about it."

"Yes, we must forget."

We went on back to the terrace. Mina and Jebb were in the bar and the floor was fairly clear, so we decided to have one more dance before I went.

3

Jebb wakened me at seven o'clock the next morning to say goodbye and to introduce me to the cleaning woman, Mrs. Choong.

"There's a fair amount of stuff in the Frigidaire," he said; "but if there's anything else you want, just write out a list and she'll do the marketing. Isn't that right, Mrs. Choong?"

Mrs. Choong nodded. "I buy for good prices. I cook, too, if you like. You want eggs for breakfast, mister?"

"Yes, please."

She was a ball of fat and the seams of her black trousers stretched almost to bursting-point as she bent down to pick up Jebb's breakfast tray. As she waddled away into the kitchen, Jebb said: "I told her you'd be sleeping in the bedroom. There are two beds there. Tell her to make both of them up if you want to. Liberty Hall, this is."

"And I'm very grateful. I can't tell you."

"Forget it, sport. Like I said, you're doing me a favour. Let's see. It's Tuesday today. I should be back Thursday night or Friday morning. When exactly do you reckon on getting away, Steve?"

"I'm hoping to get the Friday plane to Djakarta."

"Well, if they try and twist your arm too much over your exit papers, you see Lim Mor Sai and ask him to talk to his pals in the police department."

"I'll do that." It was on the tip of my tongue to tell him that the police department was not the only place where Lim Mor Sai had pals. Then, I decided not to. No doubt there were hundreds of people in Selampang who were secretly in touch with the insurgents in the north. If Lim were one of them, Jebb, as a Government employee, would probably rather not know about it. I said instead: "If you're not back before I leave, what would you like me to do about the key you lent me?"

"Leave it with Mrs. Choong. You can trust her. She's got her own anyway. But I hope I'll see you."

"So do I."

He hesitated. "She's a classy kid, Rosalie, you know," he said awkwardly.

"Don't worry. I'll do right by her. Mina's not going to be waiting for you with a hatchet."

He laughed. "Okay, sport. Sorry I spoke. By the way, if you see Lim Mor Sai, tell him I'll be bringing him some cheroots back with me. He usually asks me when

I go Makassar way. He must have forgotten this time."

"I'll tell him. And thanks again."

"If you're still here Friday, you can buy me a drink."

When he had gone, Mrs. Choong brought me a breakfast of fried eggs, coffee and papaya. Later, when I had bathed and shaved, I considered my clothes. Up in Tangga, I had seen myself making do with what I had until I reached Singapore. Now, the situation was different. My ridiculous suit did not matter; I would not be needing a jacket while I was in Selampang; but I would certainly need some more slacks and shirts. I consulted Mrs. Choong. She told me that she could get shirts *dobi*-ed for me in a few hours, but that if I wanted them properly laundered I would have to wait twenty-four. She also gave me the address of a good Chinese tailor.

I went to the tailor first and ordered two pairs of slacks and four shirts for delivery late that afternoon. Then, I paid my first call on the police department.

Sundanese officials are peculiarly difficult to deal with, especially if you are an English-speaking European. The first thing you have to realise is that, although they look very spruce and alert and although their shirt pockets glitter with rows of fancy ball-point pens, they have only the haziest notions of their duties. The language problem is also important. All the forms you have to fill up are printed in English as well as Malay, because English is an official language and the officials are supposed to be bi-lingual. The trouble is that they will never admit that they are not. If you speak in Malay they feel bound to reply in English. Unfortunately, the few words they have soon run out, and although they may continue to *look* as if they understand what you have said, they are in fact hopelessly at sea. Their technique for dealing with the resulting impasse is to pretend that they have to consult a colleague, and then go away and forget about you. The form you have completed gets lost. Your only chance is to say and write everything very distinctly both in English and Malay, and to keep fingering your wallet as if you are getting ready to pay. You are, indeed, going to have to pay eventually; and not merely the legal fee for the service in question. When the formalities are almost completed, it will suddenly be discovered that you ought to have produced another "clearance," and that without it you cannot have whatever it is you want. A Kafka-like scene ensues. Nobody can tell you precisely what this mysterious clearance is or how you set about obtaining it. The shifty brown eyes peer at you. It is your move now. You ask what the fee for the clearance would be if one knew where to obtain it. A figure is named. You ask if, as a special favour, you may deposit this sum so that when more is known about it, the clearance may be obtained for you. There is a shrug, then a grudging assent. The eyes watch sullenly as you count the money out. You agreed too quickly. He is wishing he had asked for more and wondering if it is too late. No, it is not. He made a mistake. He forgot the price of the Government stamp. You smile politely and pay that, too. There is no answering smile. Other brown eyes have observed the transaction and there will be a share-out when you have gone. To get out again into the open air is like emerging from a depression.

The granting of an exit visa to a resident European is a big operation. My first visit to the visa section of the police-department headquarters lasted an hour. In that time I managed to secure the five different forms that had to be completed, and countersigned by various other authorities, before the formal application could be submitted. This was good going. I went next to the agents for the Hongkong and Shanghai Bank, cashed a cheque and had one of the forms countersigned. After I had deposited it, together with another form, at the Internal Revenue Department, I called in at the Indonesian Consulate and applied for a transit visa. By then, it was time for lunch.

I went to the Orient Hotel, where they had an air-conditioned bar. I also hoped to find De Vries, the Sunda-Pacific Airways traffic manager, and thus save myself the trouble of calling in at his office. He was there all right, nursing a de Kuyper's gin as if it were all that he had left to live for. Sunda-Pacific Airways ran the scheduled passenger services out of Selampang under a Government franchise that was due to expire later that year. The Government had recently announced that it would not be renewed, and that a new national airline authority would take over. He knew only too well that, while international air safety requirements would necessitate their retaining the Dutch pilots, no such necessity would protect the rest of the Dutch staff. He had been one of the original members of the company. His bitterness was understandable.

After he had promised to see that a seat was held for me on the Friday plane to Djakarta, he asked me how things were up in Tangga. I told him, and asked how things were in Selampang. It was a foolish question; but I had nothing to do until the offices opened again, and I thought, somewhat virtuously, that the least I could do was to listen to him.

I received the answer I deserved.

"You know damn well how things are in this city. I would be pleased if you would stop encouraging me to become a bore. Have another drink."

Over luncheon, however, he did unburden himself a little.

"I wouldn't like a Government spy to hear me saying this," he said; "but people like me have only one chance of survival here."

"What's that?"

"A revolution."

"You mean Sanusi?"

"Why not? Did you know that he'd appointed a representative in New York to lobby the United States, and that for the past six months he's had agents in Malaya and Pakistan, meeting religious leaders and canvassing support for the movement?"

"No, I didn't."

"The censorship has been quite efficient, but in my business news gets around. I can tell you, they're badly worried down here. Sanusi controls more than half the total area of the country as it is. The Nasjah Government has failed completely. The country's bankrupt, the elections were a farce and the Communists are getting stronger every day. If Sanusi were to take over tomorrow, the Americans and British would probably sigh with relief."

"I don't see how you'd be better off, though."

"We couldn't be worse off. At least, we could come to terms with Sanusi."

"Are you sure of that?"

"Sanusi may be a fanatic in some ways, but in others he is open to reason."

"You speak as if you knew him."

"Oh yes, I know him. You forget, he commanded the garrison here." He paused, then added: "There are lots of people in this place who know Sanusi."

"I'm sure there are. Has he any weaknesses?"

"Wishful thinking. Same as me."

A waiter was hovering near us. De Vries began to

talk of other things. It was not until we were sitting on the terrace having our coffee that he reverted to the subject. A column of army trucks with troops aboard them went by. The troops were in full marching order, with steel helmets and machine pistols. They were clinging on for dear life as the trucks bounced over the pot holes outside the hotel. I remembered something I had read in the Government newspaper that morning about an important army exercise.

"Sanusi has another weakness," De Vries remarked sombrely.

"Oh?"

"He does not like to take chances."

When the Government offices reopened I made another tour, beginning with the Ministry of Public Works, who were required to certify that I was leaving the country with their knowledge and without any of their property in my possession, and ending with the police department, where I deposited the completed forms, together with my passport and a substantial sum to cover "fees." A sour police lieutenant then agreed reluctantly that, if I returned the following day at about the same time, the exit permit might be stamped in my passport. When I arrived back at the tailor's it was no surprise to find that the slacks and shirts I had ordered were ready for me; nevertheless, I was pleased. After a day with official Sunda, it was refreshing to deal with the businesslike Chinese.

Back in the apartment, I slept for an hour or so. When I awoke, I found that it had rained heavily and that the air smelt of, and felt like, hot mud. However, the water in the bathhouse was cool, and, after I had showered, I was able to dress without too much discomfort.

I had arranged to meet Rosalie at the New Harmony Club at eight thirty. Soon after eight, I locked up the apartment and set out. The lift was not working, and I had to walk down the stairs past the floors occupied by the radio station. The corridors had sponge-rubber carpets laid along them and there was a lot of external wiring on the walls; but otherwise they looked much like floors in an ordinary office building. On one landing workmen were manhandling a heavy piece of electrical equipment that looked like a meat safe out of the lift. When I reached the ground floor I could hear a big diesel generator set thudding away in the basement. The radio station, Jebb had told me, was independent of the city power supply. The two policemen on the door glanced at me casually, but did not trouble to look at the temporary pass their predecessors had given me earlier in the day.

Mahmud pedalled over grinning when he saw me come out, and soon we were splashing through the rain-filled pot holes along the Telegraf Road towards the racecourse.

I would like to be able to say that I sensed something

strange about the city that evening—an inexplicable tension in the air, a brooding calm that foretold the storm—but I cannot. Most of the drains had overflowed with the rain and added their own special stench to the normal canal smell, but there seemed to be just as many people about as there had been the previous night, and they all seemed to be behaving in the normal way. On one patch of wasteland beside the road, there was even a small fair in progress. A carousel had been set up, and a small stage on which two Indian conjurors were performing. Mahmud slowed down as we went past. One of the conjurors was holding a tin chamber pot, while the other pretended to defecate coins into it. As the coins clattered into the pot, the crowd applauded happily.

When I got to the club, I went through into the bar. It was fairly crowded, but I was relieved to find that neither Lim Mor Sai nor his wife was there. The Dutch couple were at their place by the piano. I had a drink and watched them for a time. Once, the pianist nodded vaguely to them and began to play what was evidently their favourite tune. The man touched his wife's hand, and she looked at him fondly. The man smiled and said something to the pianist; but he was bored with them again. For him, no doubt, they were merely two pathetic Europeans who drank too much and breathed across the piano at him every evening, distracting him with their tiresome adulation from his private world of soft lights, rich boy-friends and American recordings. It was all rather depressing.

Then, Rosalie arrived and things were suddenly different.

She was wearing a light cotton dress that should have made her look more European, but for some reason had the reverse effect. As soon as she saw me, she smiled and came over, nodding to someone she knew on the way. There was nothing self-conscious about her greeting, no arch pretence that she had not really expected to find me there. She was glad to see me and I was glad to see her, and, as I was drinking gin, she would drink that, too.

It was a good evening. I don't remember all the things we talked about; Mina and Jebb for a while, I know, and the police department, food, clothes, Singapore, air travel, and the black markets; but after we had dined, and then danced a bit, we talked about ourselves. I learned that she had a sister who worked for a shipping company, that her father, who had been in the Dutch army, had died in a Jap P.O.W. camp, and that her mother preferred to live now with relatives who owned land near Kota Baru. She learned that, after a spell in the Western Desert, I had spent most of the war building airfields, that my wife had gone off with a Polish army officer while I had been away, and that my firm in London had written asking me if I would like to do a job in Brazil.

Lim Mor Sai showed up later in the evening and went round the tables making himself agreeable to the customers. When he stopped at our table I gave him Jebb's message about the cigars. Just for a moment it seemed to disconcert him.

"Cigars? Ah yes. That is most kind." He paused. "May I ask where you are staying, Mr. Fraser?"

"Jebb's lent me his apartment. Why?"

He hesitated, then shrugged apologetically. "Here one always asks. The hotels are so full. You are fortunate." He bowed slightly and moved on; but I had a feeling that he had left something unsaid. So had Rosalie. I saw her look after him in a puzzled sort of way; then our eyes met, she smiled as if I had caught her out in an indiscretion, and we got up to dance again.

We left the place soon after eleven. Mahmud was waiting outside. There is just room for two reasonably slim persons in a *betjak,* and he waved away a colleague who tried to muscle in. Rosalie gave him an address, and he set off enthusiastically, the chain making cracking sounds as he threw his weight on to the pedals.

The street to which he took us was on the outskirts of the Chinese quarter. The pavements were arcaded, and between the shops there were broad, steep staircases leading to the upper floors. About halfway down the street, Rosalie told him to stop. Then she got out

66

and hurried up one of the staircases. I lit a cigarette and waited. A little way along the street, an old man was sitting on the edge of the open drain with his legs dangling into it, solemnly combing a long grey beard. On the opposite pavement there was a Sikh watchman asleep on a charpoy placed across the doorway of a furniture shop. Only two or three windows in the street showed any light. It was so quiet that I could hear Mahmud breathing.

Rosalie was gone about ten minutes. When she returned, she had a small dressing case with her. I told Mahmud to drive us to the Air House.

There, the policemen on duty at the door glanced casually at my pass and nodded. They paid no attention to Rosalie. The generator in the basement was silent; presumably, the radio station had shut down for the night. The lift was working again and lights had been left on in the fifth-floor corridor. Beyond the swing doors at the end of it, however, there was pitch darkness and I had to strike matches to light the way to the apartment. I remembered how unprepossessing it had seemed to me the previous day.

"It's not all as bad as this," I said.

"I know, Mina told me. Besides, I helped her choose the furniture."

When I had left the apartment, I had locked all the windows on to the terrace. She sat down while I opened up the living room, but when I came back from doing the bedroom, I found that she had gone into the kitchen and was looking at the refrigerator.

"Thirsty?" I asked.

"A little." She patted the refrigerator. "Does it work?"

"Oh yes."

I got a tray of ice out and showed her. She smiled and wandered off into the living room. When I went in there with the ice and glasses, however, she was out on the terrace.

I watched her. For a moment or two she stood quite still, looking round at everything as if she were making an inventory, then she walked away slowly past the *attap* screen to inspect the bathhouse. She was out of sight now, but I could hear her shoes clicking on the concrete. The sound receded and then got louder again. I heard her go into the bedroom. The sound of her footsteps ceased, and I knew that she was standing there taking in everything and getting used to it. The drinks were made, but I left them where they were and stretched out on one of the long chairs. I did not want to interrupt her.

A minute went by, and then I heard her move.

"Steven?" It was the first time she had used my name.

"In here."

She came through from the bedroom and smiled when she saw me on the chair.

"I have been looking at everything," she said.

"Yes, I know."

I handed her a drink. She drank about half of it, but thoughtfully, as if she were up against a serious problem. I asked her what it was.

"It is very warm," she explained carefully. "I was thinking that I would take a bath."

"Is that all? Well, I'm going to take one, too. You go first."

She came back from the bathhouse wearing a sarong. The towel was draped modestly over her breasts and her black hair hung loose on her shoulders. I left her standing by the terrace balustrade, looking down into the square below.

The water was deliciously cool. I dried myself slowly so as not to get warm again, tied a towel round my waist and walked back along the terrace.

She was no longer there, and there was only a single light on in the living room. It shone indirectly through the open door into the bedroom. It was there that I found her.

It was still dark when I awoke and the terrace outside was almost white in the moonlight. I knew that it was a sound that had wakened me, but I did not know what sound. I looked across at Rosalie asleep on the other bed; but she was quite still. There was a small table between the two beds and I could see the dial of my watch glowing there. It was three forty-five.

Just then I heard the sound again. It came from away along the terrace. A man said something sharply and there was a noise like a packing case being moved on concrete.

I swung my legs to the floor and stood up. My bath towel was lying between the beds and I wrapped it around my waist. If I were going to have to tackle an intruder, I preferred not to do so stark naked.

I bent over Rosalie and kissed her. She stirred in her sleep. I kissed her again and she opened her eyes. I kept my head close to hers.

"Wake up, but speak softly."

"What is it?" She was still half asleep.

"Listen. There's somebody trying to get along the terrace from one of the empty apartments. Thieves, I suppose. I'm going to scare them away."

She sat up. "Have you a revolver?"

"Yes, but I hope I won't have to use it. They're making a lot of noise. They probably think there's no one here."

My suitcase was under the bed. I got the revolver out, rotated the cylinder until one of the three rounds in it would fire when I pressed the trigger, and went over to the window.

There was a wall separating this section of the terrace from that belonging to the unfinished apartment next door, and it had iron spikes on it. I heard one of the men cursing as he tried to negotiate them. Now was the moment to act, I thought. As I had told Rosalie, all I wanted to do was to scare them away. If either of them got down from the wall, he would be cornered with nowhere to run to.

I stepped out on to the terrace.

I could see very clearly. The moon was behind me, shining directly along the terrace. A man was standing on the top of the wall astride the spikes. He was wearing an army steel helmet and a belt of ammunition pouches. As I watched, he bent down and took something handed up to him from below. When he straightened up I saw that it was a Japanese-pattern machine pistol. He held it up for a moment, regaining his balance, then he brought his other leg over the spikes and jumped.

As he landed on the terrace, I moved back into the bedroom. I was confused and scared now, but I had some sense left. I went straight back to the suitcase and dropped the revolver inside it.

"What's the matter?" Rosalie whispered.

I took her hand and held it tightly, motioning her not to speak. The soldier was walking along the terrace now, not cautiously, but as if he were uncertain of the way. Then, he came into view, the machine pistol held across his body as if he were on patrol. Rosalie started violently and I gripped her tighter. For a moment the man outside stood silhouetted in the moonlight. He looked round and stared at the bedroom window. Rosalie began to tremble. He took a step towards it.

Suddenly, a loud hammering noise came from the living room, and I realised that someone was beating on the outer door of the apartment.

The man on the terrace peered round and then went through the open window into the living room. The door into the bedroom was open and we saw him cross towards the hall. A moment later there was the sound of the bolts of the door being shot back and a murmur of voices. The lights in there went on.

I stood up. My dressing gown was lying on a chair and I tossed it to Rosalie. Then, putting my finger to my lips, to warn her to keep quiet, I walked through into the living room.

There were several voices murmuring in the corridor now. Suddenly, there was a sound of sharp footsteps approaching and the voices were hushed.

A Sundanese voice said: "At your service, Major *tuan.*"

A moment later, Major Suparto walked into the room.

4

He did not recognise me at once. His pistol holster was unfastened and his hand went to it quickly. At the same moment he called sharply to the soldiers in the corridor. As he levelled the pistol, two of them ran in through the doorway. They had the long chopping-knives called *parangs* in their hands, and as soon as they saw me they started forward with a shout.

I had opened my mouth to tell him who I was, but it all happened so quickly that I was still gagging over the words when he yelled to the two men to halt. They were within a yard of me with their *parangs* raised to strike, and their teeth clenched in the mad killing grimace. Another second and he could not have stopped them hacking me to pieces. As it was, they stood there dazed, their faces gradually regaining a stupid sort of sanity as they lowered their arms.

Suparto came towards me, thrusting them aside.

"What is this?" he demanded. "Why are you here?"

I was so unnerved that it did not occur to me that those should have been my questions. Idiotically, I started to explain about hearing someone climbing on to the terrace. He cut me short.

"The owner of this apartment is in Makassar."

"I know. He lent it to me."

He swore, stared at me bitterly for a moment and then motioned to the two soldiers to stand back.

They retreated, awkwardly as if they had been reprimanded. I was coming to my senses again now and realised that there was something unfamiliar about their uniforms. The trousers were of khaki drill, but it was not the same khaki that I had seen on other troops in the city. And both men were wearing a sort of yellow brassard on the left arm. So was Suparto.

"Are you alone?"

"No."

"Who is here with you?"

"A woman."

He moved past me swiftly to the bedroom door and went in.

Rosalie stood in the centre of the room. She was turning back the sleeves of my dressing gown. As she swung round to face him, her hands dropped to her sides, but she made no other movement.

"Your name?" he said.

"Rosalie Linden, *tuan.*"

He turned the light in the bedroom on, then looked from one to the other of us.

"You can see we're both quite harmless, Major," I said.

"Possibly. But your presence is inconvenient. Are you armed?"

"There's a revolver in that case under the bed."

He looked at Rosalie. "Pull the case out. Do not open it."

As she obeyed, he called in the N.C.O. and told him to take the revolver. Then he looked at me, his lips tightening.

"Armed men enter your apartment in the middle of the night and steal your property. Yet, you say nothing, you make no protest. Why, Mr. Fraser?"

"The men are wearing uniforms and this is Selampang, not London."

"You do not even ask questions?"

"That would be a bit pointless, wouldn't it?"

"Because you think that you already know the answers?"

I knew that it was dangerous to go on pretending to be stupid. I shrugged. "Less than forty-eight hours ago you were in Tangga, Major. You didn't come here by sea or air and those men outside are not Government troops. I presume then that they are General Sanusi's, that you are in sympathy with his aims, and that the long-awaited day has arrived. No doubt you've taken over the radio station below and will shortly begin broadcasting the good news to the rest of the country. Meanwhile, other troops are occupying the central telegraph office, the telephone exchange, the power station and the railroad station. The main body of your forces is taking up positions surrounding the police barracks, the ammunition dump, the forts defending the outer harbour and the garrison . . ." I hesitated. I had remembered something.

"Yes, Mr. Fraser?" His face was very still.

"Most of the garrison moved out today on manoeuvres."

"The moment, of course, has been carefully chosen."

"Of course. However, I'm a foreigner, and it's no concern of mine. Now that you've satisfied yourself that there is nobody up here who could possibly do anything to interfere, I take it that you will allow us to go back to sleep again."

He considered me coldly. "I like you, Mr. Fraser," he said at length; "and I am sorry to see you here. At the moment, however, I am wondering if I have a sufficient excuse for allowing you to remain alive."

"You need an excuse? We're no danger to you, for God's sake!"

"As I have said, your presence is inconvenient."

"Then let us go somewhere else."

"I regret that that is impossible."

I said nothing and looked across at Rosalie. She was still standing by the open suitcase. I went over to her, put my arm round her shoulders and made her sit down on the edge of the bed.

Suparto seemed to hesitate; then he beckoned impatiently to the N.C.O. and nodded in our direction.

"These two persons," he said, "will remain in this room. Post a sentry on the terrace. They may go one at a time to the bathhouse, but they will go by the window. This door will remain locked. If either attempts to leave without permission, they are both to be killed."

The N.C.O. saluted and eyed us sullenly.

Suparto looked at me. "You understood what I said?"

"Yes, I understood. May I ask a question?"

"Well?"

"Was I right? Is this part of a *coup d'état?*"

"The National Freedom Party of Sunda has taken over all the functions of government and assumed control of the country."

"That is what I meant."

"The so-called Democratic Government of the colonialist traitor, Nasjah, has proved unworthy of the people's confidence." He was speaking Malay now, and as if he were addressing a public meeting. Behind him, the N.C.O. nodded approvingly. "The guilty will be punished. The Unbelievers will be destroyed. Colonial influences will be eliminated. The Faithful will rally to

77

the standard of Islam. As soon as the emergency is over, elections will be held. But order must be maintained. Hostile elements will be wiped out ruthlessly."

"Do we count as hostile elements?"

"It might be thought so." He lapsed into English again. "At present the decision is my responsibility. Later, it may be different. My superior officers, who will arrive here shortly, are sensitive men and the presence of Unbelievers at such a time may not be tolerated. In your own interests, I would advise you to be as silent and unobtrusive as possible."

"I see. Thank you, Major."

"I can promise you nothing."

With a nod he turned and went out of the room. The N.C.O. shut the door and the key turned in the lock. A moment later a soldier appeared on the terrace outside the window, peered in and then sat down with his back against the *attap* screen and his machine pistol cradled in his lap.

I looked down at Rosalie and she smiled uncertainly. "Why does he like you?"

"I don't know that he really does. He has no special reason that I know of. That is the officer who was up at Tangga, the one with the jeep."

"Oh. Perhaps if you explained how discreet you had been, he would let us go."

"I don't think so. We know too much."

"What do we know?"

"That this is their headquarters. He spoke of other officers who will arrive. That'll be General Sanusi and his staff, I suppose. They knew Jebb was away. Having ear-marked this place for their headquarters, they may even have arranged that he should be. It's logical enough. There aren't many buildings in the city as strong as this one, and Sanusi would naturally want to be near the radio station. He'll be using it quite a bit, I imagine."

"Do you think that they will kill us?"

"I don't know."

"I think they will." Her tone was quite even and matter-of-fact.

"Why should you think that?"

"They kill very easily. During the war of liberation I saw them. Men like that major. They smile and then they kill. For them it is easier to kill than to have doubts, to be uncertain."

She stood up and then went over and switched off the light. Outside on the terrace, the sentry turned his head quickly. Rosalie crossed to the window and drew one of the curtains so that the man could see only half the room. He stirred, and I moved across to watch him. He was waiting to see if the other curtain would also be drawn. When it was not, he relaxed.

Rosalie had taken off my dressing gown and dropped

it on the chair. The strong moonlight was visible even through the curtains, and I could see her standing there running her hands over her body as if she had never touched it before. Then she realised that I was watching her and laughed softly.

"I saw the men with the *parangs*," she said; "and I knew that if they killed you, they would also kill me, because they would not have been able to stop. So, I was ready to die. Now, I am alive again."

I went over to her. I think I meant to make some futile apology for having brought her there, but instead I kissed her.

From far away across the city there came a sudden rattle of machine-gun fire. The sentry got up and went to look out over the parapet. We stood behind the curtain, listening. There were several more bursts of fire and one or two small explosions that might have been from mortars. After about ten minutes, the firing ceased and there was an uncanny silence. It was broken by a murmur of voices from the square below, and a series of crashes as the windows of the Air Terminal offices were knocked out. I guessed that the ground floor was being fortified against a counter-attack. Once, a truck whined and clattered along on the other side of the square, but otherwise the streets seemed to be deserted. A little before five, there was a glow in the sky from a fire which Rosalie thought might be in the neighbourhood of the police barracks, and, soon after, a single explosion just heavy enough to make the windows vibrate. It could have been a small demolition charge of some kind.

When the first bout of firing had ceased, we had feverishly hurried into our clothes, as if we had overslept and were late for an appointment. There was, I suppose, a logical need for haste; Suparto had warned us to expect further visitors; but I think that the true reason was less rational. Until that moment, what we had been facing had been like a nightmare; terrifying, yet also unreal. The sound of firing had sharply disposed of the unreality, and we were left with our fears. Our scramble for our clothes was a scramble for cover of a different sort. We wanted to feel safer. In fact, we only felt hotter. After a time, we sat on one of the beds, and smoked and listened and sweated and suffered the twin ills that afflict everyone who finds himself on a battlefield: the knot of fear in the stomach, and the desperate desire to know what is really going on.

Thanks, no doubt, to the treachery of Suparto and others like him, Sanusi's army had been able to make its approach march in secrecy, and to mount an attack at a moment when the capital was almost unguarded. Surprise having been achieved, it seemed unlikely that General Sanusi would have much difficulty in the early stages. Nothing we had heard so far suggested that he had encountered anything more than token resistance, and very little of that. Probably, he was already in complete control. The testing time for him would come when the Government forces counter-attacked; *if* they counter-attacked, that is; if there were not too many Supartos in their ranks.

I remembered the snatch of conversation I had overheard in the garden of the New Harmony Club. "We must have all," the General had said. "Then it must be delayed until the second day," had been Suparto's reply. All what? Reinforcements? Arms? Hostages? And what was it that had to be delayed? A movement of troops? The assassination of the President? The offer of an amnesty? I worried at the questions as if the answer really mattered. It was more agreeable to do that, than to reflect that what was going to happen on the second day was possibly of only theoretical interest to Rosalie and me.

It was nearly six o'clock when the sky lightened and then flushed with the sudden glow of the equatorial dawn. For the past half-hour there had been sounds of activity from the square below. Several cars had driven up and there had been sharp words of command. There had been a murmur of voices from the next room also. It had been difficult to distinguish what was said. We heard some isolated phrases: ". . . medical service . . . damage to installations . . . rice distribution . . . police situation . . . guns fire out to sea . . . transport arrangements . . . hour of curfew . . ." And then someone switched Jebb's radio on.

For several minutes there was only the crackling of static. The set was near the open living-room window and we could hear it plainly. Then, as the station carrier wave started up, the static faded and presently the usual *Soeara Sunda* recognition signal, five notes played on the bamboo xylophone, came on. Rosalie seemed to find the sound reassuring. I did not.

Whether the insurgents had forcibly rounded up the engineers and were now standing over them below with guns, or whether they were relying on sympathisers among the technical personnel was immaterial. The fact that they already had the station on the air was an impressive demonstration of efficient staff-work. If their other arrangements were working as smoothly, the possibility of an early change in the situation was remote. I wondered what had happened to Nasjah and his followers. Had they managed to get away, or had they been taken by surprise and hacked to pieces in their homes?

At six thirty the xylophone sound ceased and a man's voice gave the station identification. This was followed by the announcement, repeated three times, of an important government statement and a request to stand by. At six forty-five the same voice read out the statement.

It began with a recital of the "crimes" committed by the Nasjah Government, and then went on to say that, in order to save the nation from the colonialist vultures gathering over its helpless body, the People's National Freedom Party had taken over the functions of government. The Nasjah gang had run away. Insignificant bands of their adherents, incited by foreign agents, might make isolated attempts to resist the authority of the new government; but these would quickly be eliminated. In the capital, order had been restored and all was calm. However, as a precaution against reactionary elements and to protect life and property, certain temporary security measures had been ordered by General Sanusi, head of the People's National Freedom Party.

There followed a list of ordinances, amounting in effect to a declaration of martial law, and an intimidating series of instructions to provincial mayors. It was stated finally that, within the next few hours, General Sanusi would himself broadcast a message of hope and encouragement to the loyal people of Sunda from his secret headquarters. Meanwhile, they should stay quietly in their houses. Groups of more than three persons assembling in the streets would be treated as hostile and dealt with accordingly. Admittedly, this was harsh, but if the people were to be protected against the Godless forces of reaction, harshness was necessary. All loyal, right-thinking men would understand the necessity. Through discipline the way lay open to freedom.

The voice stopped. A few seconds later the recognition signal began again.

The sunlight was pouring on to the terrace now. At

that time yesterday I had lain half-awake on the spare
bed in the living room, trying to ignore the sounds of
traffic coming up from the square below. Today, there
was scarcely a sound. Now and again a vehicle drove up
to the Air Terminal entrance, but apart from that the
square was silent. Like a wary animal, the whole city
seemed to have gone to ground. Six floors down, in the
roadway, a soldier hawked and spat, and the noise interested the soldier on the terrace sufficiently to make
him look down over the balustrade.

"Freedom!" said Rosalie sharply. She used the Sundanese word *"merkeda"* and made it sound like a curse.

She was sitting in the chair behind the drawn curtain, the sunlight casting the pattern of the material
across her face. I could not see her eyes, but her hands
were gripping the arms of the chair tightly and her
whole body was tense.

I shrugged. "All political parties use that word." I
paused, then added: "Why don't you lie down and try
to get some rest?"

She did not answer, and after a moment or two I
went over and put my hand on her shoulder. As I
touched her, she sobbed and began to cry helplessly. I
put my arm round her and waited. When I felt that the
worst of it was over, I led her to the bed and made her
lie down. Then, I went back to the chair, took my shirt
off and wondered what it was she did not like about
freedom. In the next room the recognition signal

stopped again and the voice began to repeat the earlier announcement.

I was quite sure that she had gone to sleep, but, as the announcement ended, I heard her sigh and looked over at her.

She was watching me.

"There is something I wish to say," she said.

"Go to sleep. You will feel better."

She shook her head. "It is about my father. I did not tell you the truth. I said that he died in a Japanese prison camp. That is not true."

"Is he alive then?"

"No. He died, but not in that way."

I waited.

For a moment or so she stared at the ceiling, then she went on. "My father was in a camp in Siam. When he came back, we went outside the city to a small place where my father owned a plot of land. We thought that for us it would be safer where there were other Eurasian families, because of the way the *pemoedas* hated us."

"*Pemoedas?*"

"That is what we called the young soldiers of the liberation army. Anyone who was not Sundanese they wanted to kill. When the Amboina troops left, there was nothing to stop them. Even the police were afraid of them, or perhaps they did not care."

She paused, and then went on slowly. "One day, a lot

86

of them came in trucks. They had guns, and they made everyone in the village leave their houses and stand in the square while they searched the houses. They said that they were looking for hidden arms, but they were really looting. They took everything of value that there was and put it in the trucks. Then, one of them saw my father. Some of the other men in the village had made him stand among them so that he would not be noticed, but this *pemoeda* saw him and shouted to the others that he had found a Dutchman. The others came running up. Some of them were boys of fifteen or sixteen." She drew a deep breath. "They took my father, and tied him by the wrists to a hook at the back of one of the trucks. They said that he should stay there until there was nothing left of him but his hands. Then they drove the truck fast up and down the road and round the square in front of us. And while my father was battered to death, the *pemoedas* clapped and laughed and ran along behind the truck shouting '*Merkeda! Merkeda!*' "

She stopped, still staring up at the ceiling.

"Why did you say that he'd died in a prison camp?" I asked.

"That is something that everybody understands. Sometimes I almost believe it myself. It is easier to think of."

Her eyes closed. When I went over to her a few minutes later I saw that this time she was really asleep. The voice on the radio in the next room finished the

87

second reading of the announcement and the bamboo xylophone began again.

I needed to go to the bathhouse. I picked up a towel, went to the window and snapped my fingers. The sentry turned quickly and raised his gun.

I explained what I wanted. He said something that I did not catch; but he nodded, too, so I went along the terrace. I had left my shaving things in the bathhouse, and by the time I had finished there, I felt less depressed. I have always sympathised with those legendary Empire-builders who changed for dinner in the jungle. When I came out, I did something which I would not have done when I had gone in. Although the sentry was watching me, I walked over to the balustrade of the terrace and looked down into the square.

There were even more troops there than I had imagined; over a hundred, I thought, split up into squads of about a dozen. Rough barricades had been erected at the four entrances to the square, and the squads manning them either sat on the ground smoking or lounged in nearby doorways. Between the trees on the edge of the gardens, four machine guns had been set up covering the approaches, and parked in the centre under tarpaulins were two anti-tank guns. They looked like old British two-pounders. I had always been given to understand that Sanusi's army had no artillery of any description. Possibly two-pounders had not been reckoned as artillery; possibly the situation had changed.

The sentry was fidgeting, so I went back to the bedroom, bowing to him politely on the way.

Rosalie was still asleep. I got out some new slacks and a clean shirt and changed into them. Then, I considered another matter.

I had taken a bottle of water into the room the previous night, but most of it was now gone; and the water from the bathhouse main could not safely be drunk without boiling it first. There were bottles of drinking-water in the refrigerator; but that was in the kitchen and therefore inaccessible. And there was the matter of food. With some people fear creates a craving for food; but with most, I think, it has the opposite effect. It has with me. But I knew that, if we survived the next few hours, a moment would come when food would become really necessary. I also knew that when the men murmuring in the next room grew hungry, they would soon eat what was in the refrigerator. It would be as well to see if I could appropriate a little of it, some fruit and eggs, perhaps, before that happened.

I went to the window, beckoned the sentry over and explained what I wanted. He stared back at me resentfully. I had begun to repeat my request when, without a change of expression, he suddenly drove the muzzle of the gun he was holding straight into my stomach.

I staggered back, doubled up with pain; then one of my feet slipped on the polished wood floor of the room, and I fell forward on my knees, retching helplessly.

The sentry began to shout at me. The noise woke Rosalie. She saw the sentry standing over me with his gun raised, and cried out. That brought the men in the next room out on to the terrace.

There were two of them, both officers. While I struggled to get my breath, I was dimly aware of the sentry's voice telling them what Suparto's orders had been. As Rosalie helped me up, one of them came into the room.

He was a squat, bow-legged, dark-complexioned man with a jagged wound scar on his neck. He looked down at me angrily.

"It is ordered you stay here," he said.

I managed to find the breath to answer. "I only asked if I might get some food and drinking-water from the kitchen."

"If you attempt to escape you will be shot."

"I wasn't attempting . . ." I did not trouble to finish the sentence. I could see by his eyes now that he had not understood what I had said. If I translated it into Malay, he would know that I knew, and therefore lose face. It was better to keep quiet.

He still glowered at us though, waiting for the next move.

"The soldier did not understand," I said carefully.

He hesitated. He had got that all right and was now fumbling among his English sentences for a suitable reply. I felt Rosalie stir and gripped her arm to stop her from speaking. At last, he shrugged.

"It is ordered you stay here," he repeated, and went out on to the terrace.

"What really happened?" Rosalie asked.

I told her. She made no comment, but I could see that she thought I had been stupid. I knew it myself, now. Because I had been able to bathe and shave, because the sentry had not prevented my going to the balustrade to look down into the square, because I had been able to change into clean clothes and feel for a few minutes like a rational European, I had made the mistake of behaving like one. As a result, I had a bad pain in the stomach; worse, I had reminded the men in the other room of our existence, which was what Suparto had expressly warned me not to do.

"We can't go without water," I said defensively.

"We have water. There is still some in the bottle."

"That won't last long."

"I am not thirsty now."

"But you will be later. And hungry, too."

"Perhaps."

"Well, there you are."

"We shall not die of thirst or hunger," she said.

I had no answer for that. She was not being ironical. She was merely expressing a Sundanese point of view. In lush Sunda nobody dies of thirst or hunger; only of disease or violence. There is no winter for which to prepare, no drought to fear. The harvests are not seasonal as we understand the term. Tread a seed into

91

the warm, rich earth and shortly you will have a tree heavy with fruit. Survival is achieved not by taking thought for the future, but by manipulating as best one can the immediate present. By thinking like a European, by anticipating bodily needs instead of waiting passively for them to present themselves, I had modified unfavourably the present situation of the bodies in question.

I sat on the edge of the bed and looked down at the smear of black grease that the gun had left on my shirt. Rosalie had moved away. Now she returned and sat down beside me. She had a box of Kleenex and a can of lighter fluid that Jebb had left on the dressing table. She began to wipe off the grease.

"It seemed a reasonable thing to do," I said.

"These are not reasonable people."

"I know that now."

"Why do you think that I told you about the *pemoedas* who killed my father? I know these people. Mostly they are quiet and gentle. In the kampongs you will see a boy of twelve run to his mother and suck her breast when he is frightened or hurt. They smile a lot and laugh and seem happy, though they are also sad and afraid. But some are like those madmen nobody knows about, who have devils inside them waiting. And when there are guns to fire and people to kill, the devils come out. I have seen it."

"Do you think that Major Suparto has a devil?"

"Perhaps. But he does not wish to kill you. I do not know why. But his advice was good. If they do not see you or hear you, they do not think of you, and you are safe."

I said nothing. In the silence, the sound of the radio xylophone in the next room became distinct again. The five notes were in the form of a scale. *Doh-ray-me-soh-lah*. What was the name of it? The pentatonic? Ah yes. If only they would play it descending for a change; or play the Japanese National Anthem; that used the same scale. After all, it was the Japanese who had originated the signal.

It ceased abruptly. I waited for the announcement to begin again. There was a long silence. The men in the next room were no longer talking. The sentry was staring at the living-room door. Then, there was the hiss of a disc recording surface and a rendering of the Sunda battle song. This was different from the Republican National Anthem, which was a westernised song, composed, it was said, by the Dutch saxophone-player who led the Orient Hotel orchestra. The battle song was chanted by male voices to the accompaniment of drums, many small cymbals and one cumbersome string instrument that was twanged like a zither. Gedge, who was interested in such matters, said that the battle song was not really native to Sunda, but had been imported from the Spice Islands. However, in Sunda it was supposed to evoke memories of the old warrior sultans and the

93

early struggles against the colonial powers. The reason it had not been used as a national anthem was that, even to the most sympathetic western ears, it had no identifiable melody, and a national anthem that could only be played in Sunda would, it had been felt, cause the Republic's representatives abroad to lose face.

The noise went on for three or four minutes. During it, I glanced at the sentry on the terrace. The battle song did not seem to have evoked any patriotic emotions in him; he was busy lighting a twig-like cheroot. When the music stopped, however, he looked up expectantly.

The announcer came on and gave the station identification twice. There was another pause, then another man began to speak. He announced himself as Colonel Roda, Secretary of the National Freedom Party and new Minister of Internal Security. Shortly, he said, we would hear the voice of the new Head of the State. General Sanusi, he went on, was a great patriot, a true son of Islam, who had fought against the colonial usurpers in the name of the Republic, believing that by doing so his country would be made free to follow its destiny as a political unit, and at the same time conform to the forty-two precepts of An-Nawawi. So, he had attempted to serve the Republic. But evil men had made it impossible to serve as Allah had commanded that a man should serve, with his whole heart. Questions had arisen in his mind. He had taken to his heart the first precept, which stated that actions are to be judged only in accordance with intentions. The intentions had been plainly bad. Therefore the actions were bad. He had gone further. He had examined the men at the heart of the Republic with eyes unclouded by alcohol. He had turned to An-Nawawi again for guidance and there, in the sixth precept, had been the knowledge he had sought. "Is it not a fact," the holy man had written, "that there is in the body a clot of blood, and that if it be in good condition, the whole body is also?" Certainly! And was it not also written that if the clot of blood be in a rotten condition, so also was the whole body? Was not that clot of blood the very heart? Indeed, yes. Therefore, the heart must be purified. With other true Believers he had taken to the hills to prepare for the act of purification that had now been accomplished. As a result, a new era of peace, discipline and happiness had come to Sunda. Let all offer prayers for the author of this good fortune, *Boeng* General Kamarudin ben Sanusi.

There was a brief pause, a moment of rapid whispering, and then Sanusi began to speak.

He had a soft, pleasant voice which he used slowly and deliberately, as if he were none too sure of the intelligence of his audience.

He began by recalling the high hopes with which the Republic had been founded, and went on to describe the way in which the Nasjah Government had falsified those hopes. Power without Godliness had led to corruption. Corruption had led to the breakdown of the democratic machinery set up by the Constitution. Unconstitutional action had become necessary if the country were not to fall into anarchy, and become dominated, either by more powerful neighbors, or by the forces of colonialism which still threatened all the young nations of South-East Asia. And when the safety of the Republic was threatened, there was no time for legal quibbling. If your brother's house caught fire while he was working in the fields, you did not wait until he returned so that you could ask his permission before you poured water on the flames. If a hungry leopard came looking for food in your village, you did not call a council meeting to discuss what should be done.

And so on. It was, in effect, the speech of every military dictator who seizes political power by force of arms, and seeks to justify himself.

He went on to proclaim the suspension of the authority of parliament (until such time as it was considered advisable to order new elections) and the establishment of a new People's Army of Security (*Tentara Keamanan Ra'jat*), recruiting for which would begin immediately. All young men should offer their services. A delegation of the National Freedom Government was already in New York awaiting orders. Today it would be ordered to request recognition of the new

Government from the United Nations. Prompt recognition would be sought also from friendly Indonesia, and from the other powers represented at the Afro-Asian Conference at Bandung.

Finally, there were the carefully worded threats. The transfer of power which had taken place had been swift and complete. Inevitably, however, a few small areas remained in which, through lack of efficient communications, control was not yet fully established. Inhabitants of such areas were cautioned against giving aid to disaffected political elements, or to troops still bearing arms against the newly constituted Government of National Freedom. Reprisals would be taken against villages committing such offences against the new military ordinances, and collective fines would be imposed. All troops and police were required to signify their adherence to the new Government forthwith. Failure to do so would be interpreted as a hostile act. Terms of a political amnesty would shortly be announced, but no mercy would be shown to those whose loyalty was suspect. He concluded: "The killing of a true believer is not lawful but for one of three reasons: that he is an adulterer, an avenger of blood, or because he offends against religion by splitting the community. Remember that. But if a man shows himself faithful, then, so far as I am concerned, his life and property will be protected. His only account will be with Allah Ta'ala. Long live our glorious country!"

The battle song was played again. The men in the next room began talking excitedly. I looked at the time. It was eight o'clock. Less than twenty-four hours earlier I had been told that Sanusi was a man who did not like to take chances. Now he was the head of the state. I wondered what sort of man he really was.

There was one thing I did know. The voice of Sanusi was not the voice of the General I had heard talking to Suparto in the garden of the New Harmony Club two nights ago.

5

Ten minutes after the end of the speech there was a stir in the next room and talk ceased. In the quiet that followed, I heard Suparto's voice out in the corridor. Then, there were footsteps and the door of the apartment closed. A moment or two later, Suparto and two other men walked out of the living room on to the terrace.

I had never seen a picture of Sanusi, but he had been described to me once and it was not hard to recognise him. In a country where maturity is reached early and the average expectation of life is low, a man of forty-eight is almost elderly and generally looks it. Sanusi did not. The close-cropped hair showing beneath his black cap was grey and his cheeks were cadaverous, but his body was lean and muscular and he moved with an alert grace that was anything but elderly. His companion, whom I took to be the sanctimonious Colonel

Roda, was plump by comparison and had long black hair bulging from under his cap. I could not see his face. His uniform shirt was soaked with sweat and he was carrying a leather document case.

Suparto followed them over to the balustrade, and waited while they looked out over the city. Sanusi was smoking a cheroot, and after a moment or two he pointed with it down into the square and said something which I did not hear. There was no hint of triumph in his attitude, no suggestion that he found it pleasant to contemplate the city he had conquered; he was simply a military commander casting an eye over his defences.

Rosalie was getting worried by my standing so near to the window. The sentry could not see me because I was hidden from him by the one drawn curtain, but she was afraid that if the men further along were to turn round suddenly, I should be seen watching them. I knew that she was right and moved away.

It was as well that I did so, for almost immediately they began to move along the terrace in our direction. I saw the shadow of the sentry move as he straightened up.

"An ultimatum," Roda was saying; "surrender of the forts within an hour on reasonable terms or total destruction. Surely, *Boeng* . . ."

"No." It was Sanusi's voice and, as he spoke, the footsteps ceased. "They will surrender anyway when they are hungry enough. But if you offer them terms now and they refuse, you will have to attack. We shall certainly lose men and I cannot spare them. In any case, it does not trouble me. A few stupid gunners shut up in forts with guns they cannot point at us. Let them stay there until they starve. What is important is to find out what we have to expect from the enemy at Meja. Which way are they moving? Which of their units can we be sure of? These are the uncertainties I do not like."

They began to move towards us again.

"We know the units loyal to you, *Boeng*." This was Suparto.

"We know those who promised loyalty, but how many will commit themselves to us before the result is certain?"

"All," said Roda.

"If we had only one plane for reconnaissance . . ." Sanusi began and then broke off. He was level with the bedroom window now and had seen the sentry. "Why is this man here? We do not need him."

I took Rosalie's hand.

"He is guarding two prisoners, *Boeng*," said Suparto evenly. "They were in the apartment when it was requisitioned for your use."

"Prisoners? Are they hostile?"

"No, *Boeng*. But it would be unwise to release them yet. Your whereabouts must remain secret at present."

"That is true," said Roda. "There must be no failure of security. That is Suparto's responsibility. The enemy would be glad to talk to such people."

"Who are they?"

"One is an Engishman. He has been the consulting engineer up at the Tangga River dam. He is a good technician and an employee of the Colombo Authority. I thought that you would wish him to be treated with consideration."

"You said two prisoners," put in Roda.

"The other is a woman, an Indo"—he used the slang term for Eurasian—"from the New Harmony Club."

There was a silence. Rosalie's hand lay absolutely still in mine.

"The apartment," Suparto continued, "is owned by an Australian pilot. He had lent it to the Englishman. Admittedly, it is a disagreeable situation."

"They should have been handed over to the troops for disposal," Roda said irritably. "If . . . ." He paused.

In the next room the telephone had begun to ring. One of the men there answered it. The call was for the General.

Sanusi turned away to go into the living room. "The matter is unimportant," he said; "it can be considered later."

A moment or two after, we heard him curtly answering the telephone. I looked at Rosalie. Her whole body was rigid.

"You see, now," she whispered; "I am the danger to you."

"Nonsense."

"It is always the same when there is trouble. There must be someone to blame, someone to hate. The Chinese are too powerful and would combine together. But nobody cares about the Indos because we are weak. Besides, I am here with you. That will make them want to kill. They will say that I have made this place unclean, and there will be a pleasure for them in the killing."

I managed to smile. "Oh now, wait a minute. I don't think it's as bad as that. What you say might be true of some of them, but Sanusi's not a savage."

"A good Moslem does not speak as he does."

"I wouldn't know. He sounds reasonable."

"And Colonel Roda?"

"I expect he does what he's told. And you heard Suparto. He doesn't want us harmed. In any case, they're all going to have far too much to do to trouble about us. They may not even stay here. This is only a tactical headquarters. If things go on as they're going now, Sanusi'll soon be moving into the Presidential Palace. We'll be able to laugh at all this."

"You are very kind to me."

"Kind?"

"You know very well that if I were not here there would be no great danger for you."

It was she who was smiling now, faintly, as she watched my face. I got up impatiently and lit one of my dwindling supply of cigarettes, but I knew that she was not deceived. Neither was I. I had heard the change in their voices when Suparto had told them about her. For these men, with their desperate pride of race and hatred of Europeans, she already stood for treachery; and the fact that she was there with me made the iniquity of her existence doubly obscene. To kill us both might seem like an act of purification. Everything depended, really, on how necessary such an act might become to them. And that in turn depended on events. I had been right, I felt, about one thing. If things went well, Sanusi would be quick to install himself in more becoming surroundings. We would be forgotten. What we had to fear was a set-back to their plans.

I went as near as I dared to the open window. Sanusi was still on the telephone. Occasionally he would ask a question. "How many?" "Who is in command?" Evidently, he was receiving a report. Probably, it concerned the dispositions of the "enemy's" forces about which he had expressed so much uneasiness. I thought again of De Vries and his assertion that Sanusi was reluctant to take chances. There might have been something in that after all. Was it Colonel Roda who had tipped the scales in favour of the move? Or Suparto?

The telephone in the next room tinkled as Sanusi hung up. At the same moment, I became aware of a faint throbbing sound. For a moment, I thought that it was something to do with the radio station below. Suddenly, the sentry outside shouted: *"Kapal terbang!"*

The men in the next room hurried out on to the terrace. I could hear the planes clearly now, and it sounded as if there were several of them. There were shouts from the square below. Colonel Roda began pointing up into the sky.

I looked round. Rosalie was sitting passively on the edge of her bed. I blundered over to her, grabbed one of her arms and dragged her down with me on to the floor.

From where I was lying, I could see through the open window on to the terrace. There was nobody standing there now. Then, I saw the planes. They were coming in over the north-west corner of the square; three old twin-engined American fighter-bombers, flying in a ragged line-abreast formation at about twenty-five hundred feet. As they roared overhead I could see extra bombs in the racks below the wings. The whole Republican Air Force, or, at least, all of it that could get off the ground, was out.

The bow-legged officer ran on to the terrace and gazed up after the planes. Rosalie started to get to her feet. I pressed her back on to the floor. It was possible that the Air Force was throwing in its lot with Sanusi, in which case the planes would be going in to land at the civil airport out by the racecourse; but it was also possible that they were not. The behaviour of the men on the terrace had not suggested that they were expecting such a welcome reinforcement. The low altitude and steady course of the planes might simply mean that their pilots knew that there were no ground defences for them to worry about, and that they had time to make their bombing runs carefully. If there were going to be any bombing, of course; if this were not just a threatening gesture.

A moment or two later, I knew that it was not. The sound of the engines which had almost died away was beginning to get louder again, and the bow-legged officer hastily retreated into the living room.

After Sanusi's broadcast, I suppose it was inevitable that the Government would make some attempt to put the radio station out of action; but when it came, the attempt was still a very unpleasant shock. In war it is relatively easy to be philosophical about being bombed or shelled indiscriminately; but when you become, or the building you are in becomes, a selected target for enemy fire, things are different. It is not just that the degree of danger has changed; quite often it hasn't; but that the affair is no longer impersonal. From being a man like yourself, dutifully scattering high explosive where it seems likely to inflict the most casualties, the enemy has suddenly become a vindictive maniac intent on your personal destruction. You become resentful, and begin, most sensibly, to think of ways of killing him first. There is nothing more enraging than to have to stay where you are, a passive, stationary, impotent target, and let him take pot shots at you. That is what it was like at the top of the radio building.

They came in one after the other in line-ahead, and just high enough to avoid bomb blast from the ground. As I heard the first one beginning his run, I realised that there were big glass window panes two feet from our faces, and dragged a rug from the floor over our heads. At the same moment, someone down in the square opened up with a machine gun.

The sound of the plane became suddenly louder and there was a series of slithering noises as the bombs started to fall. Then, the explosions came. He must have let go everything he had, for the floor bucked and trembled for close on ten seconds. There was a pandemonium of falling plaster and breaking glass and then, as a sort of finale, a torrent of earth and stones poured down on to the terrace.

One of the bombs had fallen into the garden of the Ministry of Public Health next door, and the earth and stones were merely the falling débris of that explosion; but, of course, it sounded as if the building were collapsing. Rosalie cried out and there was a yell from the terrace. I flung back the rug and saw that the sentry was still at his post outside the window, crouching against the balustrade under the bamboo sun roof, which had collapsed. He had been hit by the roof when it fell, and was gingerly rubbing his shoulder. The curtains had been sucked out by the blast and were now caught up on the open window frame, but the glass was still intact and so was the ceiling. The blast damage was probably on the lower floors. Then I heard the second plane on its way, and dived under the rug again.

The first stick of bombs had straddled the Air House, and it was just as well that the pilot in question had no more bombs. He was too accurate. Next time, he might have scored a direct hit. The second stick was wide and ploughed along a street running parallel to our side of the square. It made a lot of noise and a few more windows went in the rear of the building; but, as far as we were concerned, that was all. It was the third plane that did the most damage to the sixth floor. Most of its bombs fell in the square, but one of them hit the portico of the Ministry of Public Health. We did not know that until later, however; at the time, it seemed like a direct hit on our own building. It was not a big bomb, but it exploded on a level with the second floor and most of the blast came our way. The floor heaved. Something hit me hard in the back. Then, there was a long, low rumbling and silence. I became aware of a thin, high singing in my ears.

My right arm was across Rosalie's shoulders and I could feel her trying to get up. I went to fling back the rug and found that there was a weight pressing on the top of it. That made me panic. I struggled to my knees and fought my way out of the rug. Suddenly, I choked, and then began coughing as I breathed in a cloud of plaster dust. I still could not hear properly, but I knew now what had hit me in the back. It was a large piece of the ceiling.

I dragged the rug off Rosalie and helped her to her feet. She was white with dust and coughing helplessly. I led her over to the bed, dragged a sheet of plaster off it and made her sit down. My ears were still painful, but the drums in them were beginning to function again. I could hear coughs and hoarse shouts coming from the next room. Through the cloud of dust, I saw that the windows had shattered and that the curtains were hanging in ribbons. I started to cough again, and, at the same moment, I heard the planes returning. Then, one of them opened up with his cannons and roared overhead.

I don't think Rosalie even heard it; in any case, she was too dazed to respond to the sound. I did nothing. I guessed that, finding their target still standing, they were trying to shoot up the radio masts. However, they had no ammunition that would penetrate the rein-forced concrete roof over our heads; and, with most of the ceiling down and the windows gone, there was nothing more they could do to us.

They made six runs in all and, from what I heard,

only managed to hit the roof twice. They were not very good at their jobs. Then, at last, having circled a couple of times to inspect the results of their work, they flew off.

The plaster had begun to settle now. I gave Rosalie a towel to wipe her face with, and then I went to the window.

The first thing I saw, lying on the terrace amid the broken glass, was the sentry's machine pistol. I peered through the tattered curtains looking for its owner.

He was sitting on the concrete with his head lolling between his knees, and blood pouring from a deep gash in his neck. I called to him sharply. He raised his head slightly and then sagged over on to his side.

I dragged a sheet off my bed, rummaged in my suitcase until I found a razor blade, and went out to him.

Something had hit him on the head, almost knocking him out; there was blood coming from just above his right ear. Probably, he had been flung against the balustrade by the blast. The cut in his neck, however, had been done when the windows flew to pieces. A piece of the glass was still sticking in the wound. Something had to be done about that. I cut through the hem of the sheet with the razor blade and then tore the material into strips. With one strip I made a pad. Then, as gently as I could, I eased the glass out of the wound. It bled a little more profusely, but not much more so. I clapped the pad over it, and then began to bandage it into place. He did not utter a sound. He scarcely moved. Once, when I pulled the glass out, he opened his eyes and looked at me, but he was no longer really interested in what was happening to him.

Feet crunched on the broken glass behind me, and I looked round.

The bow-legged officer was picking his way across the terrace towards me. He was covered from head to foot in plaster dust and there was blood trickling down his forehead.

"It is ordered you stay in," he said.

I went on with the bandaging. He went to the living room and called for two men. They came running out, and he told them to look after the sentry. They stood over me while I finished tying the bandage, but made no attempt to stop me.

When I stood up, they hauled him to his feet and helped him away. The officer picked up the gun.

"He has a head wound," I said. "He should have medical attention."

"You go in." He levelled the gun at me, but without very much conviction. He was a stupid man, and the fact that I had helped the sentry had evidently confused him. I decided to take advantage of the fact.

"It is still permitted to go to the bathhouse?" I asked.

He hesitated, then nodded.

I went into the bedroom and told Rosalie that she could go and wash the dust off. She was still shaken, but the prospect of a bath made her feel better. As she went along the terrace, I saw that the bow-legged officer was posting a new sentry. The dust had made me intolerably thirsty. While the officer was still there, I asked again for a bottle of drinking-water and some fruit. He seemed to take no notice; but a few minutes later, while I was trying to clear up the mess in the room, the sentry appeared at the window and put a bottle of water on the floor and a bowl of fruit beside it.

I thanked him. He grinned, shrugged, made a gesture of cutting someone's throat, and, with another grin, pointed to me. I grinned back and he went through the pantomime again. Then, he explained it in words. "Man's throat cut, man cannot eat, food fall out." A comedian, this one. I smiled until my jaw ached.

Rosalie, when she returned, was impressed. The fact that they had remembered my request meant, she said, that they were ashamed of their earlier behaviour, which meant in turn that they did not hate us too much. I did not tell her that I had asked again in order to get the fruit and water; nor did I tell her about the new sentry's little joke.

We ate half the fruit and drank a third of the water. I was still filthy from the plaster dust. When the rest of the fruit and water had been put away to keep cool, I got permission from the sentry to go along to the

112

bathhouse and clean up. There, I found that the water supply was no longer working. It did not matter at that moment. The Dutch ewer was full and there was a further supply in the storage cistern on the roof, but I could hear that there was no more water coming in.

As I walked back along the terrace, I was surprised to see Rosalie at the window talking to the sentry. When he heard me coming, he smiled and moved away.

Rosalie's eyes were gleaming with excitement.

"Why did you not tell me that you helped the man who was wounded?" she began, as I went back into the room.

"It didn't seem important."

"It has made a very good impression. That man is his friend. He told me he would bring us more fruit later."

"You mean they've decided not to kill us after all?"

"Oh no, but now they do not hate us so much."

"That's something, I suppose."

"He told me that there are machine guns being mounted on both sides of the roof in case there is another air attack, also that the Nasjah army is advancing from the direction of Meja."

"How does he know that—I mean about the army?"

"He heard one of the officers on the telephone. It is curious," she went on thoughtfully; "before, that man would not have looked at us except to think how it would feel to kill us. Now, because you bandage his friend, it is different. He speaks to us and brings us fruit."

"That's because of the bombing, and because we were all covered in dust just as he was. He's not used to air attack. He was frightened, and now because he isn't dead he feels generous and friendly and wants to talk. It's nothing to do with my bandaging his friend. It always happens. Besides," I added, "you're a woman. That would make a difference, too."

She thought for a moment or two and then nodded. "Yes, I understand. It was the way I felt when the men with the *parangs* did not kill us last night. I wanted you to take me to bed at once. If it had not been for the guns beginning to fire and making me frightened in another way . . ."

I kissed her, and she smiled. "Was it like that in the war?" she said. "When you had been very frightened of being killed or wounded and were not, did you always want a woman afterwards?"

"Well, there wasn't much to be frightened of building airfields, and when we were in the desert there weren't any women to have."

"But you would want one?" she persisted.

"Oh yes. There was nothing to stop you wanting."

"Now you are making a joke of it. I think it is very good that people should feel that way."

"There's a simple biological explanation."

"Is it biology that I am here with you?"

"Well, not exactly."

"No. It is because it is good for a man and a woman to have pleasure together. If they are sympathetic, that is . . ."

"And if they aren't being threatened by men with *parangs,* and bombed, and peered at by sentries."

She looked startled, but did not turn her head. "He is watching us now?"

"With great interest."

Without once letting her eyes stray in his direction, she walked over to the window and looked up at the torn curtains. "If you will take these down," she said, "I will pin the pieces together. Then we can put them back again as we wish. If we do it now, he will think it is because of the sun. If we wait until the sun has moved, he will know that we do not wish to be seen and will be offended."

"All right."

It was a good idea in any case. The sentry had managed to hoist the bamboo roof back into position, but the blast and débris had split it in several places, and the sun was pouring through the gaps into the room. Every slight movement raised the dust again, and even the sight of it swirling about in the shafts of sunlight made me thirsty.

I made a great show of shielding my eyes from the glare as I unhooked the curtains. The sentry, squatting in one of the patches of shade, watched idly while Rosalie, with the few pins and a needle and thread that she had in her case, tacked the pieces of curtain together. When I put them up again, I was able to cover almost the whole of the window space.

Since the air attack, the telephone in the next room had been in constant use, but the voices had been those of the junior officers. I had concluded that Sanusi, Roda and Suparto had temporarily abandoned the sixth floor for some less exposed command post. When, as I finished rehanging the curtains, I heard footsteps crunching towards us over the broken glass on the terrace, I assumed that it was the bow-legged officer on his way to the bathhouse. Then, the footsteps ceased, the curtains were brushed aside and Major Suparto stepped into the room.

I saw Rosalie freeze into the passive immobility with which she had faced him before, but he did not even glance at her. He looked at the ceiling, at the débris piled in one corner of the room, finally at the curtains.

"Aren't these repairs a waste of time, Mr. Fraser?"

"I don't think so."

There was no trace of plaster dust on his uniform. I guessed that he had been in the corridor when the ceilings of the apartment had come down.

"The planes may be returning soon," he said.

"They will have to score a direct hit to do any more

damage here. And I understand that you are putting machine guns on the roof. If they couldn't manage to hit the place before, they're not likely to do better when they're under fire."

"I hope you're right, Mr. Fraser. Now, I am sorry to disturb you, but you must come with me."

The knot in my stomach tightened. "Where to?"

"I will show you."

"Both of us?"

"Only you."

"Shall I be coming back here?"

"I am not taking you to be executed, if that is what you mean. If you behave intelligently it is possible that you will be sent back here. Now, please."

Rosalie had not moved. There was nothing I could do to reassure her. I pressed her arm and followed Suparto out on to the terrace. He turned into the living room.

The sentry stared blankly as I crunched past him.

The living room was in a wretched state. No attempt had been made to clear the rubble. Two pictures were lying on the floor. Some of the chairs had gone.

There were three officers there, one of them on the telephone. Suparto stopped and addressed himself to the bow-legged one.

"Nobody is to go into the next room unless this Englishman is there," he said. "Is that understood?"

"*Ya, tuan.*" He eyed me curiously.

Suparto nodded to me.

I followed him out into the passage, past a sentry and down the stairs to the next floor. There were two more sentries on guard at the swing doors. As Suparto approached they stood aside for him to pass.

The ceiling had come down in the corridor beyond, and some of the doors belonging to the offices leading off it were propped against the walls. Just beyond the main stairway landing, a group of officers stood outside an office door listening to a captain reading out orders for the requisitioning of rice. They made way for Suparto and I followed him through an office, where a man sat loading machine-gun magazines, to a door marked "TECHNICAL CONTROLLER." Suparto knocked on the door and went in.

There were three men in the room: Sanusi, Roda and a man in civilian clothes whom I recognised as the editor of a Selampang newspaper subsidised by the Nasjah Government. I had met him when he had visited Tangga with a party of other journalists; but if he now remembered me, the memory was inconvenient, for he gave me no more than a blank stare. Sanusi and Roda were reading a copy of a printed proclamation which was spread out on the desk. Suparto and I stood just inside the door, waiting. When the reading was finished, there was a muttered conference between the three men, and then the editor took the proclamation away. Sanusi looked at me.

"Mr. Fraser, *Boeng*." Suparto prodded me forward.

I went up to the desk. Sanusi examined me thoughtfully as I approached, but it was Colonel Roda, sitting at the corner of the desk, who spoke.

"You are an engineer?"

"Yes."

"At Tangga Valley?"

"I have been resident consulting engineer there for the past three years."

"Then you are a fully qualified and experienced person, no?"

I did not hear this properly for the first time. He spoke English with a Dutch accent, but it was his determination to be peremptory that made it difficult to understand. He had broad, fleshy lips, and the words rattled about in his mouth like pebbles.

"I beg your pardon, Colonel."

He repeated the question loudly and even less articulately, but this time I got the meaning.

"Yes, I am qualified."

"Then you will consider yourself under the orders of the National Freedom Government. Any delay or negligence in the carrying out of such orders will be punished immediately by death. Major Suparto . . ."

"A moment, Colonel." It was Sanusi who had spoken.

Colonel Roda stopped speaking instantly, his eyes alert and respectful within their nests of fat.

Sanusi considered me in silence for several seconds, then he smiled amiably. "Mr. Fraser is a European," he said; "and Europeans expect high payment for their services to natives. We must fix a good price."

Roda laughed shortly.

"Were you paid a good price in Tangga, Mr. Fraser?"

"Yes, General."

"And yet you hope to leave us?"

"A man must return to his own country sometimes."

"But what is a man's own country, Mr. Fraser? How does he recognise it?" He still smiled. "When I was a child here in Sunda and worked with my family in the fields, I did not know my country. If we were near a road and a Dutchman came by, or any European, my father and mother had to turn and bow respectfully to him. Us children, too. It was the Dutchman's law and, therefore, the Dutchman's country. Are you married, Mr. Fraser?"

"No, General."

"The woman with you. Is she a Christian?"

"I don't know, General."

"There are three fine Christian churches in Selampang. Did you know that?"

"Yes, I knew."

"And the Buddhist and Brahmin places of worship, they are also very fine. Have you seen them?"

"Yes."

"Tell me, where are the mosques?"

I hesitated. Roda laughed again.

"I will tell you," Sanusi continued; "one is by the cattle market, the other is by the Chinese fairground. They are small, decayed and filthy. They are insults to God."

He was probably right; but I could not see what it had to do with me.

"And yet President Nasjah wears the cap." He touched his own significantly. "And so do the members of his Government. Which mosque do they go to for prayer? The cattle market or the fairground? Or do they worship in the toilets of the Presidential Palace?"

I stood there, woodenly.

"They say they won our independence as a nation from the Dutch," he went on. "They lie. It was the Japanese forces who defeated the Dutch, and the forces of circumstance that gave us our independence. But the hands of Nasjah and his gang were there to receive it, and so they seemed to the people like great men. The people are loyal but misguided. We have no great men. Under the Dutch, no Sundanese was permitted to rise in the public service above the rank of third-grade clerk. So now we have an administration controlled by third-grade clerks, and a government of petty thieves and actors. We are corrupt, and only discipline can save us from the consequences. To you, to any European, that much is certainly obvious. But it will not come from outside. Not from China, not from America. It will come from what is already in us, our faith in Islam. Of that you may be sure. Meanwhile, we need help. That we must ask help from Europeans and Unbelievers is humbling to us, but we are not vain men."

There was a pause. Some comment seemed to be expected of me.

"What is it you wish me to do, General?"

"A trifling service. Major Suparto will explain."

"One of the bombs that fell in the square just outside damaged the main water conduit," said Suparto, evenly. "The lower basement of this building was flooded and the generator equipment which supplies the power for the radio transmitter has been put out of action. It is necessary that it should be repaired immediately."

"But I don't know anything about generators."

"You are an engineer," snapped Colonel Roda.

"But not an electrical engineer, Colonel."

"You are a technician? You have a university degree? And are there not generators at Tangga?"

"Yes, but . . ."

Sanusi raised his hand. "Mr. Fraser is a technician and also a man of resource. That is sufficient. For a suitable inducement he will lend us his skill. Yes, Mr. Fraser?"

"It's not a question of inducement, General."

"Ah, but it is." His smile faded. "This woman, *Van*

der Linden, whose religion you do not know, does she please you?"

"I like her, yes."

"To us her presence is offensive," he said. "Perhaps, if you do what is required, you will persuade us to tolerate it."

"I've tried to explain, General. It's not a question of whether I want to help you, or don't want to. It's just that I don't happen to have the right kind of knowledge. There must be someone in this city better qualified to help you than I am."

"Coming from Tangga, you should know better than that, Mr. Fraser. Obviously, if there were a technician here better qualified to repair the damage, we should use him. But we have no one available, and work must begin at once. You must be ingenious. You must acquire the knowledge."

"With all due respect, General, you don't know what you're talking about."

Roda sprang to his feet with an angry exclamation, but I took no notice of him. "I'll see what I can do to help," I went on; "but, for goodness' sake, leave Miss Linden out of it."

Sanusi stared at me for a moment, then shrugged. "Certainly, if you wish. What is it you want instead?"

I did not immediately understand what he was getting at, but from behind me Suparto spoke quickly. "Mr. Fraser did not mean that, *Boeng*. If he is successful, he will hope that the woman's presence may be tolerated, as you suggest."

"Ah, good." Sanusi glanced at Roda. "For a moment, Colonel, I was afraid that what happened to his woman was of no interest to our engineer."

Roda chuckled. He had seen the joke coming.

Sanusi looked up at me. "We understand one another?"

"Yes, General."

"Then there is no more to be said." He nodded dismissal. "God go with you."

I went.

6

S uparto led the way back to the stairway and we
began to walk down.

"Was this your idea?" I demanded.

"No. It was the General's."

"Do you agree with it?"

"I am not in a position to agree or disagree. But I
think he has had worse ideas."

I glanced at him, but he did not seem to be aware of
having said anything odd.

"What's the extent of the damage?"

"That you will have to discover for yourself. There
are two of the station engineers below. Perhaps they
will be able to help you."

"Station engineers? Why can't they do the job themselves?"

"That is a polite way of describing them. They know
how to operate the transmitter, which switches to press,

which dials to turn, but they are not technicians. They know nothing about the generator except how to start it."

"But somebody on the staff must know."

"Possibly, but we have only certain members of the staff with us. The sympathisers."

"You're in control of the city. Can't you round up the others?"

"The three senior technicians are all Chinese. We have sent patrols into the Chinese quarter with instructions to find the men, and they may eventually succeed. But not today, and perhaps not tomorrow either. The General cannot wait."

"Why not? What's so important about the radio? I shouldn't have thought that there were very many people in the country with short-wave receivers."

"It is not the people inside the country who matter to the General. It is the impression outside that he is concerned about. Later today, he proposes to broadcast again in English. His speech will be addressed to the cities whose good opinion matters most to him at the moment: Djakarta, Singapore, Canberra and Washington. The speech, part of which you have already heard, will be issued to the world press correspondents here at a special conference afterwards."

"What do you mean, 'part of which I have already heard'?"

"Surely you did not believe that so much eloquence

could be unrehearsed? 'To you, to any European, that much is certainly obvious.' Come now, Mr. Fraser, admit it. You must at least have wondered."

He was smiling slyly at me. It was an invitation to share a joke and I distrusted it deeply.

I said non-committally: "I had other things to wonder about."

"Ah yes. But you see why it is so important that the station should be working properly. If the General does not speak to the world, the world may think that he cannot speak, that he is not yet really in control and that they had better withhold their gestures of friendship until they see more clearly who has won. The General attaches great importance to the power of radio propaganda. He believes that it can be of decisive political importance." There was a distinctly critical note in his voice.

I said: "And you do not?"

"I think that the realities of power are important, too."

"You make the General sound a bit naïve."

"Not naïve, Mr. Fraser. Simple, like all great men."

We had been picking our way down the rubble-strewn stairs. Now we were at the ground floor. In the hall there were troops stacking rice sacks half-filled with earth to make a blast screen. The elevator gates were open and a man's body in a police uniform lay across the threshold in a mess of congealed blood. I caught a glimpse of his face as we came down the stairs. It had been one of the guards who had passed Rosalie and me into the building the previous night.

Suparto stopped and shouted for the N.C.O. in charge of the sandbagging. The man came running and Suparto told him to have the body taken outside. As the man went off to carry out the order, Suparto looked after him unpleasantly.

"They are animals," he said.

We started down the stairs to the basement. From below there came a sound of voices and a smell of fuel oil and drains. On the landing halfway down, I stopped.

"May I ask you a question, Major?" I said.

His face became impassive. "About what, Mr. Fraser?"

"Last night you were good enough to say that you liked me. I have been wondering why."

His face cleared. "Ah, I see. You wish to assess the value of my friendship, the extent to which it might be relied upon and used. Well, I will explain. You remember the day I arrived in Tangga with my colleagues?"

"Very well."

"We were stiff-necked, presumptuous, and arrogant. I most of all, because I did the talking. There were reasons, but"—he shrugged—"we will not discuss them now. You had reason to be annoyed, and you *were* annoyed with me, were you not?"

128

"A bit."

"You made it plain. But it was the way in which you made it plain that impressed me. You did not say to yourself: 'Here is another of these tiresome little brown men, these pathetic little upstarts in uniform, whom I must pretend to treat respectfully in order to show that I do not think of him as an inferior human being.' You did not patronise, as Mr. Gedge does, and you were not more tactful than was necessary. You dealt with me frankly as you would have dealt with a European in the same circumstances, and there was no calculation in your attitude. You treated me neither as a dog, nor as a pet monkey who may bite. And so I liked you."

"Oh. Well, that's very civil of you. But it wasn't to assess the value of your friendship, as you put it, that I brought the matter up. What I wanted to know was if you would trust me."

"With what, Mr. Fraser?"

"A confidence. Which side are you really on, Major? The National Freedom Party's or the Government's?"

"Naturally, Mr. Fraser, I am on the side of the General. How could you doubt it?" He smiled easily.

"I don't, Major. But which General do you mean?"

For once, I saw him disconcerted; but it was a short-lived pleasure. His lips narrowed and his hand went to his gun.

"You will explain that remark," he said softly.

"Certainly. I was in the garden of the Harmony

Club two nights ago. I saw your jeep. I knew it came from Tangga. I knew it could only have come by road, so . . ."

"How much did you hear?" he demanded abruptly.

"Not much, but enough to know that there are two Generals in this. Who is the other one?"

He ignored the question. "Whom have you told?"

"Nobody. It wasn't my affair."

"You said nothing of this last night."

"Why should I? Until I heard Sanusi's voice I thought that he was the other man whom you called 'General.'"

"Was Miss Linden with you?"

"She only saw the jeep. She heard nothing."

"I can believe you?"

"Yes."

He sighed. "But why do you risk your life by telling me?"

"Because I want to save my life if I can, and Miss Linden's. If what I suspect about this business is true, I don't think either of us has very much of a chance. Do you?"

He looked me in the eyes. "Nobody here has very much chance."

"By showing you that I can be trusted not to betray you, I increase what chance we have."

"How?"

"If you can help us, you will."

"Why should I help you? A moment ago, I was on the point of shooting you like a dog."

"You will help me because, if the occasion arises, you can trust me to help you. Also, because you are a humane man."

He stared at me grimly. "I would not depend too much on my humanity, Mr. Fraser. It may still become necessary for me to shoot you."

"If it becomes necessary, of course, you will. I said that you were humane, Major. I didn't accuse you of sentimentality. Now, you'd better show me this generator."

We went on down the stairs.

"One thing I should like to know, Mr. Fraser," he said. "Is your ignorance on the subject of generators as complete as you claim?"

"I have a certain amount of theoretical knowledge, naturally, but I don't think that's going to be much use. If the windings are damaged, and they probably are, there's nothing I can do."

"I ask, because if the generator is not running again by sundown, I am afraid that harsh disciplinary measures may be taken against you. I would regret that, but I could do nothing to stop it. And now, here we are."

We had come to a short flight of steel stairs leading down to the sub-basement. There were lights on below and at the foot of the stairs there was a gleam of black, oily water. There were sounds of splashing. The bottom

131

two stairs were under the water. Suparto went down as far as he could without getting his feet wet and called sharply.

There was more splashing and then two bedraggled young men waded to the foot of the stairs.

"What progress?" Suparto asked curtly.

One of them shrugged. "The water is no longer coming in, but we cannot make the drain work."

"The *tuan* here is an engineer from Tangga. He understands these matters. You will take orders from him now. Mr. Fraser, these men are Engineer Osman and Engineer Alwi."

I nodded to them and made my way down to the water level. From there I could see the whole area of the room. It was about thirty feet by twenty. The generating set and two five-hundred-gallon fuel tanks occupied most of the space. The diesel part of the set stood clear of the water but the generator itself was half-submerged. To one side was a slate switchboard.

I looked at Osman. "You say that there is a drain that won't work."

"Yes, *tuan*. We have put rods down it, but it will not work."

I looked at Suparto. "How close did the bomb fall?"

"In the roadway at the side. You wish to see the crater?"

"No. But what happened?"

"The crater filled up with water from the broken

pipe before a man who knew how to turn the water off could be found. Then it was found that the water was coming in here."

"Where did it come in? A crack in the floor? Down the walls? Where?"

"Up through the drain, *tuan.*" This was Engineer Alwi, wide-eyed with wonder. "It bubbled up through the drain. I saw it."

"Then what the Hell's the good of poking about trying to get it to run back *down* the drain?" I demanded. "Don't you see what happened? The bomb collapsed the drain conduit as well and the water from the crater took that way out. We must be below the crater here. Naturally the water won't run back uphill. We'll have to pump it out."

"What do you need, Mr. Fraser?" This was Suparto.

"A powerful rotary pump. A fire-truck would do the job, or maybe there's a sewage-disposal unit. Any pump that will lift water twenty feet at a reasonable speed. There's nothing to be done until we get it."

But Suparto was already hurrying up the stairs. Osman and Alwi stood there in the water looking at me sheepishly.

"Where does the exhaust from the diesel go?" I asked.

"There is a pipe, *tuan,*" said Osman. "It comes out at the back of the building."

"There must be a ventilator shaft. Where is it?"

"There in the corner, *tuan*."

"Where does that come out?"

"I don't know, *tuan*." He wrung his hands. "How should I know?"

"All right, Osman. Don't worry. Just go upstairs and see if you can follow it. It looks as if it may come out where we can reach it from the outside. You understand? Then, when the fire-truck comes, we can run the hose down through the ventilating shaft and reach the water that way. It will be quicker."

"Yes, *tuan*." He was smiling eagerly as he clambered out of the water and squelched away up the stairs.

I was left with Alwi. He was waiting attentively for his orders. It occurred to me suddenly that all I had to do was to invent some task for him that would take him out of sight for a few minutes, to be free to walk out of the building. It was unlikely that anyone would try to stop me. If anyone did, I could say that I had gone to inspect the ventilator. If all went well, I could be at the British Consulate in ten minutes. True, my passport was at the police department awaiting an exit permit; but providing that I was not stopped by a patrol, that would not matter. I would be safe.

When the day-dream was over, I sat down on the stairs and wondered idly if Suparto were counting on my reluctance to abandon Rosalie to keep me from escaping, or whether he had preferred to rely upon more direct methods.

"Alwi," I said, "a guard should have been posted at the top of the stairs to prevent unauthorised persons interfering with our work. Go and see if he is there."

He looked a bit mystified, but he went readily enough. I lit my last cigarette. He was back before I had taken two puffs.

"The guard is there in position, *tuan*."

Suparto was, after all, a realist.

"Very well," I said. "Now tell me. Was the generator set running when the water came in?"

"Yes, *tuan*. There was a loss of power. My colleague, Osman, came down and found the water. The motor stopped running as he came in."

"Did any fuses blow?"

"We have not looked, *tuan*."

I lowered myself into the water and waded over to the switchboard. The generator set itself had been made by the Krupp engine works at Kiel, but the board was Japanese. There was a "no-volts" circuit-breaker on it and that had tripped. After a bit, I discovered that the motor control box was linked to the circuit-breaker. It seemed likely that the motor was undamaged and that it had cut out automatically as a result of the electrical failure. No fuses had blown. It was possible, I decided, that the generator windings had not burnt out and that the loss of power had been due simply to the damp insulation; but it would be a long time before I knew for certain one way or the other. There was one other hope, a faint one.

"Can't you adapt the equipment to use the mains power?"

Alwi looked at me reproachfully. "But that is direct current, *tuan*. One hundred and thirty volts."

So that was that.

It was eleven thirty then. Soon, Osman came to report that he had found the ventilator shaft opening and that it was near enough to the ground to serve as a duct for the hose pipe. There was an extractor fan fitted to the basement end of the shaft. So that there should be no delay when the pump arrived, I told them to get some tools and remove the fan. When that was done, we sat on the stairs and waited.

Just before noon there was another air raid. This time the target seemed to be on the outskirts of the city. Presumably, the fact that the radio station was no longer on the air had satisfied them. Down in the sub-basement we could feel the concussion of the bombs. The lights flickered once, and Alwi said that it must be the power station that was being attacked; but, to my relief, the lights stayed on. About ten minutes later, Suparto arrived, accompanied by a terrified fireman wearing a steel helmet, and reported that a motor pump was outside.

I sent Osman up to show them the ventilator shaft.

At twelve thirty they started to pump. There was a delay when Suparto noticed that the water was being allowed to run back into the bomb crater; but after another hose had been fitted to carry the water from the pump to a drain farther along the road, the work was uninterrupted. By one fifteen, the water in the basement had sunk to the level of the intake hose nozzle, and further pumping was impossible. There was still an inch or so of water on the floor, but it was well clear of the generator housing and could be dealt with later.

Suparto was looking pleased. "You must admit, Mr. Fraser," he said sportively, "that the General's methods sometimes produce results."

"What results?"

"You have made progress."

"We haven't even started yet."

I called for a hand lamp and made a careful inspection of the generator. This told me nothing that I did not know already. The thing was designed to deliver alternating current at five hundred volts, and the windings were soaking wet. I also knew there was only one course open to me; that was to dismantle the thing, dry the windings out as best I could, reassemble it and hope to God it worked.

Suparto was standing over me, watching expectantly. To get rid of him I explained that I should want heating appliances of some sort, preferably blow lamps, a couple of electric fans, some thin sheet iron and a block and tackle. When he had gone to give the necessary orders, I began, with Osman and Alwi, the dismantling process.

In one of the ceiling joists there was a ring bolt that had obviously been put there to lower the generator into place when it had been originally installed. I managed, eventually, to get a rope sling round the armature; then, by using the block and tackle rigged to the ring bolt above, I was able to sway the armature clear of the housing. But the job took well over an hour. The coupling to the generator had proved all but inaccessible, and we had had much more dismantling to do than I had anticipated. We had, moreover, removed the fan from the ventilator shaft to get the hose through, and the heat down there became overpowering. By the time we were ready to start drying out, we were too exhausted to go on without a rest.

Suparto had food brought to us—*nassi goreng* and fruit—and we squatted on the stairs while we ate. I got some cigarettes, too. Suparto watched us keenly, like a trainer; with us but not of us.

"What about Miss Linden?" I asked him. "Has she had any food?"

"I will see that she gets some."

"And drinking-water, and cigarettes?"

"Very well." He looked at his watch. "It is three hours

to sundown, Mr. Fraser. It will be necessary soon for me to report to the General."

"I can't tell you a thing. I shan't know whether it's going to work until we're able to try it."

"He has called a press conference at the Presidential Palace for six. There, he will distribute copies of the proclamation; also the radio address he expects to deliver tonight. If the radio is not working he will be exposed to serious humiliation."

There were a number of replies I should have liked to have made to that; but Osman and Alwi were listening. They were looking worried, too.

"Well, we'd better get on with it," I said.

My plan for drying the windings was simple; it had to be. What I did was to bend the sheet metal into two big tubes, wrapping wire round each one to hold it together. Then I kept the sides of the tubes heated by the blow lamps and blew air through them with the fans. They were, in effect, like two large hair-driers. One I set up to blow into the field windings inside the housing. The other I directed at the armature suspended in its sling from the ceiling. Neither of them was very efficient, as a lot of the heat was wasted; but I could think of no better way of doing the job.

There were two blow lamps to each tube, and, once their most effective positions had been determined, all we had to do was to keep them going. The atmosphere rapidly became stifling, but we had time to replace the ventilator fan now, and when that was set going, things improved. After a while, I momentarily switched off the fan blowing on to the armature to feel if the ropes round it were getting too hot, and was rewarded by the sight of a whiff of steam rising from the windings.

At about four o'clock there was another air raid, and Suparto went up to find out what was happening. To us, it sounded as if the planes had returned to the same target as before, and I was terrified lest they should succeed in cutting off the power supply to the fans; but this time the lights did not even flicker. Osman and Alwi said, gleefully, that it was because the enemy were such timid pilots, but I was not so sure. Isolated, easy to identify and, doubtless, undefended, the power station was a much simpler target than the Air House. If they had really been after the power station, I thought, even those pilots would have been able to hit it. When Suparto returned he was blandly uncommunicative; however, I was beginning to know him, and I thought I detected a hint of satisfaction in his manner. For him, at any rate, things might be going according to plan.

At five o'clock we turned off the fans and the blow lamps and began the task of reassembling. The windings felt dry outside, but that meant little. Even if there were nothing else wrong with them, there might still be enough damp inside to break down the insulation. I should have liked to cook them longer, but Suparto would not allow it. I tried to persuade him that it was better to have a generator that did work at seven rather than one that did not work at six; but he merely shrugged.

I could see why, too. From his point of view, it did not matter whether the generator worked or not; all that mattered was that the verbose, ridiculous but dangerous Sanusi should continue to trust him until it was too late to withdraw from the trap that had been so carefully set. Sanusi had ordered me to repair the generator by sundown. For my sake, Suparto hoped that I would succeed in doing so; but if I failed, he had no intention of sharing the blame with me. As a loyal servant of the Nasjah Government, a patriotic *agent provocateur*, his responsibility was to the other General, the one he had been with in the garden of the New Harmony Club, the General who was now on his way to close the jaws of the trap, and liquidate Sanusi and his National Freedom Party once and for all.

The reassembly went far too well for my liking. I wanted difficulties and delays; I wanted to postpone the moment when the whole thing would be started up and I should know for certain that I had failed. But Osman and Alwi worked with feverish efficiency. Every part fitted neatly into place first time; every nut went on to every bolt as if it had been machined by an instrument-maker; Osman even began to sing as he worked. When I told him to stop it, he giggled happily.

At a little after five thirty, we were ready to test. I held the no-volts circuit-breaker trip plate into position, closed the circuit and told Osman to start up.

The diesel fired within about ten seconds. When it was up to speed, I let the trip plate go. It dropped instantly, the breaker flew out with a bang and the diesel chuffed to a standstill.

There was a horrified silence. I thought that Osman was going to burst into tears. Suparto raised his eyebrows.

"Well, Mr. Fraser?"

I took no notice of him. I was not so worried now; I knew that there was power there, because I had seen the meters kick. There just had not been enough to hold the circuit-breaker in.

I nodded to Osman. "Start up again."

When it started this time I kept my finger on the trip plate and watched the meters. The voltage was all over the place and I guessed that there was still a lot of damp in the windings; but the probability now was that the heat of the diesel and the heat generated in the windings themselves would gradually complete the drying-out process; either that, or the insulation would break down disastrously. I kept the trip plate up. After about twenty minutes' running the voltage had steadied appreciably. I gave it another five minutes and then tried releasing the plate. It held.

Osman grinned.

"Is it all right?" Suparto asked.

"I think it may be. It's not delivering anything like full power yet, but it'll improve, I think."

"The General will be pleased. I congratulate you, Mr. Fraser."

"The rest of this water ought to be mopped up. The drier the air in here, the better."

"That shall be attended to." He glanced at Osman and Alwi. "One of you had better stay here to supervise the work. I will send men down."

"I will stay," said Osman. "Alwi should test the transmitter."

I was covered in grease and filth from head to foot, my shoes were full of water, my muscles ached and my legs were trembling. Suddenly, I felt so tired that I had to go over to the stairs and sit down.

Suparto followed me. "Are you sick, Mr. Fraser?"

"No, just tired. I didn't have much sleep last night, you may remember."

"But not too tired to report to the General, I hope?"

"Can't you report to him?"

"It will be better for you and for the woman if you speak to him yourself."

"All right."

Alwi had already gone ahead. Suparto and I mounted the stairs slowly. When we reached the guard on the stairs, Suparto told him to report back to his N.C.O.

143

The man followed us up to the ground floor, where Suparto made arrangements for the sub-basement to be cleaned up. The lift was working again now. It was the kind you operated yourself. When we were inside and the gates were closed, I asked Suparto about the air raids we had heard below.

"Were they trying for the power station?"

"No. The road and rail bridges over the river east of the city."

"Did they destroy them?"

"They damaged them badly enough."

"Badly enough for what?"

"Enough to prevent a retreat to the hills before the city is completely surrounded."

"Doesn't he realise that?"

Suparto pressed the button for the fifth floor and the lift started up.

"The General and Colonel Roda place a more optimistic interpretation on the attacks. They see them as a move to delay the Government troops who have mutinied, and who are on their way to join us here in the city."

"That interpretation having been suggested by you, I take it?" When he said nothing, I asked: "Have any Government troops, in fact, mutinied?"

"The loyalty of one infantry unit was considered doubtful. It was disarmed yesterday."

The lift stopped and we got out.

The General was preparing to leave for the foreign

press conference at the Presidential Palace, and I had to wait in the outer office. While I was there, a station monitor speaker in the corner began to emit a frying sound and then the xylophone signal came on. Alwi had got the transmitter working again.

When the General appeared at the door of his office, I saw why I had been kept waiting. He had changed into a clean uniform and was wearing a tie. Roda and Suparto followed him out.

I stood up and the General came over to me. He nodded graciously; his thoughts were already in the Presidential Palace.

"Major Suparto has told me of your hard work," he said. He glanced at the monitor speaker. "We can hear for ourselves that it has been successful, eh, Colonel?"

"As we expected, the *tuan* was too modest about his qualifications." Roda grinned.

I ignored him. "I am glad to have been of service, General."

"Sunda has need of good engineers," he replied; "especially those of proved loyalty. It is my intention to set up intensive technical training schemes for the youth of our country. For a man like you, Mr. Fraser, there might be exceptional opportunities for advancement here."

"You are very kind."

"Those who serve us well will be well rewarded. Do not forget that, Mr. Fraser."

"I have every reason to remember it, General."

"Ah yes. We made a bargain. It shall be kept."

Roda grinned again. "Deal gently therefore with the infidel,' " he quoted facetiously; " 'and grant them a gentle rest.' "

Sanusi frowned at the blasphemy but continued to look at me. "By this time tomorrow, Mr. Fraser, I shall have moved my headquarters and the security considerations which have compelled us to detain you here will no longer apply. You and the woman will then be free to leave. You agree, Major?"

"Of course, *Boeng*." Suparto's face was completely impassive.

"Meanwhile, the Major will see that your detention is not made too disagreeable."

"Thank you, General."

"We keep our promises, you see."

With a proud lift of his chin, he strode on out of the office. Roda, with a nod to me, followed.

Suparto looked at me. "You see? It was as well that you reported yourself."

"Was it? I can see why you find them easy to despise."

He shrugged. "At least you will get a comfortable night's sleep."

He led the way out of the office. We went back along the corridor, through the swing doors and up to the apartment.

The man by the telephone was asleep. The bow-legged officer kicked him to his feet as Suparto entered.

Suparto looked round, then went over to the radio and switched it on. The announcer had begun to read a communiqué issued by National Freedom Party headquarters claiming that calm and order had been restored in all provinces. Suparto switched it off again.

"This morning," he said, "an enemy bomb damaged the radio power supply. At the request of *Boeng* Sanusi, the *tuan* here repaired the damage and restored the power. Our *Boeng* has congratulated the *tuan* on his loyalty and skill, and given strict orders that both he and the woman with him should be treated with the greatest politeness and respect. They will remain in this apartment, but a guard on the terrace will no longer be necessary. Is it understood?"

There was a murmur of agreement. Suparto walked over to the drink table, picked up a bottle of whisky, and went out on to the terrace.

I followed.

Outside the living-room window he stopped and called the guard over. When the man came he dismissed him.

"You will not be so foolish as to try to leave the apartment, I hope, Mr. Fraser?"

"All I want to do is to rest."

He put the bottle of whisky into my hand. "We have no use for this," he said; "perhaps it will help you to sleep."

147

He turned on his heel and went inside again.

I walked along the terrace.

Rosalie had heard our voices and was standing by the window waiting for me. As I approached, she switched on the light.

My appearance must have been a shock to her; it was a shock even to me when I saw myself in the mirror; but she did not say anything. She was waiting for me to make the first move.

I put the bottle down and kissed her. She held on to me for a moment, then she smiled.

"I heard what the Major said. Was it true?"

"More or less. Anyway, we have a reward. We are to be treated with consideration. You see, the sentry has already gone."

"Does it mean they will let us go?"

"Well . . ." I hesitated. "Not yet. I'll tell you about it in a minute. I must clean myself up first."

She was watching me closely, and I knew that I was not going to be able to pretend to her for very long. I turned away as if to take my shirt off and saw that there were bowls of food and fruit on the table.

"You haven't eaten," I said. "I asked them to send it up for you."

"Do you think I would eat when I did not know what had happened to you?"

"The rice will be cold," I said stupidly.

She did not answer. She was still wondering what it was that I had not told her. I looked round the room.

148

In some way she had managed to get rid of the plaster dust and rubble and make the place tidy. I wanted to comment on the fact, but I could not get the words out.

I sat down on the edge of the chair and started to unbutton my shirt. As I did so, she knelt down in front of me and took off my waterlogged shoes. I fumbled with the shirt. My fingers were scratched and sore, and one of the buttons caught in a loose thread. In a weak rage I tore it free. She looked up, and then, with a murmured apology, began to help me. Every stitch of clothing I had on smelt of oil and sweat and dirty water. When I had undressed, I gathered it all up and threw it out on to the terrace.

She smiled. "While you are bathing I will get out some clean things."

Luckily there was still plenty of water left in the bathhouse; I had to soap myself several times from head to foot before I could get rid of the smell of oil.

When I got back to the room, she had switched off the top light so that there was not so much glare, and had put the bedside lamp on. There was a set of clean clothes ready for me on my bed, and also a neatly folded batik sarong.

"I can wash some of our clothes," she explained, "but I cannot iron them. You have only those white trousers clean and two more shirts. There are some of Roy's things there, but they will not fit you. Perhaps it is foolish to think of such things now but . . ."

"No. You're quite right. Anyway, a sarong will be

more comfortable. Up in Tangga I often wore one."

"You do not object that it is one of mine?"

"Object? It's a beauty."

She watched me critically while I put it on.

"There are, perhaps, more suitable materials for a man," she said at length; "but it does not look effeminate."

"Good. Have you another one for yourself?"

"Oh yes. But while you were not here and the guard was outside, it was better that I looked as European as possible. In batik I look more Sundanese."

"Then look Sundanese."

She smiled, and, going to the other end of the room, began to take off her dress. In the next room they switched on the radio.

I opened the bottle of Jebb's whisky that Suparto had given me, and poured out two drinks. I drank one straight down. Then I refilled the empty glass and took it over with me to my bed. The bruise on my stomach was beginning to be painful and I lay down gingerly. When I was stretched out flat, however, the muscles began to relax, the pain went and a delicious drowsiness began to steal over me. In the next room a voice on the radio was announcing that General Sanusi would shortly address a message to the world. I closed my eyes.

There was something moving against the fingers of my right hand and I half opened my eyes. Rosalie was gently removing the glass that I had been holding. Her hair was down over her shoulders, the sarong was fastened at her waist and she had a narrow scarf draped loosely over her breasts like a country woman. She looked beautiful. I remained still and watched while she placed the glass gently on the bedside table. Then, she glanced at me and saw that I was not asleep. She smiled and sat down on the edge of the bed. I took her hand.

"There's something I'd better tell you," I said.

"I know, but you are very tired. Sleep first."

"Sanusi said that by this time tomorrow he would have moved his headquarters, and that we would be free."

"And does he not mean it?"

"Oh yes, he means it, but there are things he doesn't know."

"Tell me."

"He's in a trap. It was all a trap; the garrison leaving the city unprotected; promises from men he thought he could trust that they would bring over their troops to his side; assurances that the country was waiting for his leadership, appeals to his vanity, warnings that if he hesitated he would be lost; anything to trick him into coming down from the hills with all his men so that the Government tanks and guns could move in and cut him to pieces. Well, it's worked. Tomorrow he thinks that he'll be moving over into the Presidential Palace.

He won't. He'll be fighting for his life, here, and I don't imagine that he has any chance at all of winning."

She had been looking down at my hand. Now, her eyes looked into mine. "How do you know this? Who told you?"

"You may be better off if you don't know."

"Major Suparto." It was a statement, not a question. I said nothing.

"They might still get away to the hills."

"Not very many of them. And none from this building, I think. They know where Sanusi is, all right."

"It will be bad again for us here."

"I'm afraid it will."

She took my hand and, leaning forward over me, held it against her breast so that my fingers touched one of the nipples. I felt it harden, and she smiled.

"You see," she said, "I am not afraid."

She pressed my hand, and then moved away. "You must sleep now, and I think I will sleep, too."

She lay down on her bed and stared up at the ceiling. I watched her face for a while, and then my eyes closed. After a moment or two, I heard her say my name.

"Yes, Rosalie?"

"Perhaps we should wear our clean clothes tomorrow."

7

The attack on the city began just before dawn. I thought at first that it was the voices of the men in the living room that had awakened me. Some sort of argument was going on, and another man was speaking on the telephone. He kept repeating the word "impossible." The argument seemed to be about someone named Dahman who had moved his troops without authority.

Then, I became aware of an irregular thudding that sounded as if, somewhere in the building below us, the wind was slamming a heavy padded door. Only there was no wind.

I opened my eyes and saw Rosalie standing by the window. There were lights flaring in the sky behind her. I sat up and gasped as I realised how sore my body was. She looked round. I got off the bed carefully and went over to the window.

Rosalie was looking over towards the bay. As I joined her, two cones of orange flame stabbed the darkness there. The sound took about three seconds to reach me, and, as it thudded against the windows, there were two more flashes. This time I caught a momentary glimpse of the shape behind them, and knew why the forts commanding the sea approaches to Selampang had not surrendered to Sanusi. The Sundanese navy consisted of only five ships: one lighthouse tender, three small patrol vessels and the flagship, an elderly destroyer which the Government had bought from the British and re-named *Semangat*. I had seen her in Port Kail. She had four 4.7-inch guns.

She was firing into an area to the left of the racecourse, and you could see the flashes of the bursts reflected on the smoke drifting away from earlier ones. Rosalie said that the barracks were in that direction.

"What should we do?" she added.

"There's nothing we can do."

She came back with me and we lay together on my bed, listening. Two men from the next room had gone out on the terrace now and were discussing the situation in low tones.

"What will happen?" Rosalie asked.

"I don't know enough about it. I suppose these people have established some sort of defence line on the outskirts. If so, the other side, with their tanks and guns, will find the weakest spot and blast their way through.

This naval bombardment is just the preliminary soften-
ing up. I suppose it's meant to impress the civil population, too. But it's the tanks and guns that will decide the
thing. Unless Sanusi has tanks and guns to fight back
with, there's nothing he can do to stop them. I'm
certain he has no tanks."

"Has he guns?"

"There are a couple of anti-tank guns down in the
square. I suppose he has a few more dotted about the
city. I don't know how old the Government tanks are,
but unless they are very old indeed, the shot that those
guns fire won't even knock a dent in them. They might
stop a light armoured car, but nothing heavier."

"What will happen, then?"

"That depends on how hard these people fight."

"But you said they cannot win."

"I don't think they can. It's only a question of how
long it takes to defeat them."

She was silent for a moment, then she said: "To kill
them all, you mean?"

"Most of them, anyway."

"They might surrender."

"They might, yes. Let's hope they will."

"Yes, let us hope." She must have guessed from my
tone that I did not think that there was much likelihood of it. The Government were certainly not going
to let Sanusi get out of the trap once he was in it, and
Sanusi would not be such a fool as to believe in any

promises they might make. Besides, when street-fighting began and men began to kill at close range, it became difficult to surrender.

I was remembering a Fusilier sergeant I had met in Burma. It was some weeks before we went into Mandalay. My company had been clearing a forward airstrip and were waiting to be flown out to another job. This sergeant had come out from the Eighth Army in Italy, and because we had both been in the desert with Auchinleck, we had started talking. He had had experience of street-fighting against the Germans, and had later become an instructor on the subject. He had developed a passion for it that even he, I think, suspected to be a trifle unhealthy. All the same, he could not wait to get into Meiktila and try his skill on the Japanese.

"It's an art, sir, rushing a building," he had told me eagerly; "a bleeding art. They can't stop you if you know how. You just have to get near enough first. That's the dodgy bit. There's usually plenty of cover, though, shell holes, ruins and that, but you've got to have patience. Crawl, dig your way there if you have to, but don't start until you're within thirty yards of a window. Then go mad. Put a four-second grenade in first and follow it. By the time you're there they'll be wetting themselves, if they've got anything left to wet with. Then, you go through the whole house. Quick as lightning. Every room. First a grenade, and then yourself. Doesn't matter what's there. Doesn't matter who's there. Then, comb it out with your machine pistol. If it's a soft house, put a burst up through the ceiling and catch them bending. But don't stop for a second. Be as quick as lightning. First a grenade, and then yourself with the old machine pistol, trigger happy. Don't be afraid of anything. They're more frightened of you than you are of them because you're attacking. Blind 'em and then hit 'em with everything. And when you run out of ammo, still keep going while they're dazed. Knife, shovel, the lot! Keep going and there's nothing that can stop you, sir. I've seen it. I've done it. I know."

I felt sure that he did know.

The sky lightened, and then the sun rose.

We went to the window again.

A pall of smoke hung over the area where the barracks were. The destroyer had ceased firing and was lying there innocently on the smooth, sparkling surface of the bay. There were some bursts of light automatic fire and one or two faint thuds that might have been two-pounders in action. The radio in the next room had been switched on. The station was transmitting a recording of Sanusi's "foreign policy" speech of the previous night, translated into Hindustani. I realised that the station had probably been transmitting in various languages all through the night, and wondered vaguely what sort of output Osman was getting from the generator. Down in the square there was a sound of trucks being started and driven off.

157

"I am hungry," Rosalie said.

"So am I."

We divided the cold rice between us and then ate some fruit. While we were eating, the destroyer's guns opened up again, but this time we took no notice. I thought that I could imagine what was going on. In the darkness their shooting had not been too good. As a result, when the tanks and infantry had moved in, they had met with more opposition than they had expected. The guns had been called upon to put down some properly observed fire before the attack was resumed. I told Rosalie this fiction as if it were fact.

She said: "How do you know?"

"That is how these things happen. Soon, the General will issue a communiqué. He will say that an enemy attack on the outer defence ring was beaten off with heavy losses to the enemy and at practically no cost to the defence. But he will also announce a tactical withdrawal to previously prepared positions of greater strength, in order to straighten the line."

"What does that mean?"

"It is the language of retreat. We shall be having plenty of it soon, I think . . ."

We both heard the planes at the same moment. As we dived for the floor, one of the men on the terrace began shouting orders to the machine-gunners on the roof. I started to drag the rug over our heads and then, remembering that there was no glass left to worry

about now, dropped the rug and pulled the curtains
aside.

"There," said Rosalie.

I saw them then. They were the three planes which
had bombed us the previous day, but now they were
flying at over six thousand feet. There was a noise like
a pneumatic drill over our heads as the machine guns
on the roof opened fire, and a few more bits of plaster
fell from the ceiling. They had one of the things
mounted almost directly above us. As the gunner trav-
ersed, a shower of ejected cartridge cases came tinkling
down on to the terrace. The gunners must have known
that, at that range, they could not have hit a house, but
they went on firing just the same.

Something began dropping from the planes. It
looked for a moment like a load of incendiaries. Then,
the black dots in the sky seemed to split up and stop
falling, and I realised that it was leaflets that were being dropped. The men in the next room realised it at
the same moment and ran out on to the terrace, staring
up and exclaiming excitedly.

The Sundanese Air Force may not have been very
good at hitting its targets with bombs, but with leaflets
it was superbly accurate. A minute after the drop, the
sky above the Van Riebeeck Square was filled with
them, evenly distributed and fluttering down in perfect
formation. Suddenly, the men on the terrace began running about wildly, capering up and down, snatching at

the air as the first of the leaflets came within reach. It was a fantastic spectacle. Two of them, intent on the same leaflet, cannoned into one another as the paper swooped capriciously over the edge of the balustrade. There were shrill cries of protest, and Rosalie began to giggle uncontrollably.

We were still on the floor and she hastily crawled away to the bed to smother her laughter. I stayed by the window, and, some seconds later, about a dozen leaflets fell on the terrace. One was within a yard of me and, when I saw that the men were not picking all of them up, I reached out and got it.

The same message was printed on both sides in Malay and English. Rosalie had recovered now and I took it over to show her.

It was not long. It was addressed: *"To All Loyal Citizens of The Republic of Sunda."* It said:

"During the past thirty-six hours, a terrorist criminal organisation calling itself the People's National Freedom Party, and led by a former officer named Kamarudin b. Sanusi, has taken advantage of the absence of the Republican Army on manoeuvres to occupy certain public buildings in Selampang and other towns in the Southern Provinces, including newspaper offices and premises used by Radio Sunda. Statements put out by the terrorists, both by radio and in certain newspapers, indicate that it is their intention to attempt, in contravention of the provisions of the Constitution of the Re-

public, to overthrow the elected Government of the Republic by force. By my lawful authority as President of the Republic, a State of Emergency has, therefore, been stated to exist, and the said Kamarudin b. Sanusi and his associates are declared to be enemies of the Republic.

"Under the Public Security Law of 1948, any person giving aid to a declared enemy of the Republic or permitting such aid to be given by others, may be punished by death. The Army of the Republic will now proceed to administer justice. The innocent, who have nothing to fear, will welcome their defenders. It is likely, too, that there are some persons who now regret their part in the disorders that have taken place. Providing that they surrender immediately to the advancing troops and give them all assistance, such persons will be treated leniently. This applies also to members of the so-called T.K.R., or People's Army of Security. Failure to obey promptly all orders issued by, or in the name of, the Officer Commanding the Army of the Republic, General Ishak, will be an offence punishable by death. We fight for Freedom and the Constitution."

There followed the printed signature of President Nasjah and the date. The ink smudged off on my fingers. Presumably, they had been printed in Meja during the past twelve hours; but someone had had the forethought to have stereos of the signature ready in advance. In dealing with its enemies, at least, the Government could be efficient.

I remarked on the fact to Rosalie. She shrugged.

"No doubt there are others like Major Suparto. It is said this swine Ishak is intelligent. What do you think that they will do to us before they kill us?" It was said quite evenly, but there was something in the tone of her voice that should have warned me to be careful. It did not, however; I was re-reading the leaflet.

"To us?" I said vaguely.

"Of course. It says that we are criminals now."

"What do you mean?"

She pointed to the leaflet. "You have helped them with the radio. I am with you. We have taken part. We shall not be able to surrender. Perhaps it will be better if we are killed here."

"Let's hope we won't be killed at all."

"Hope? That is amusing, I think."

"There's not much else we can do."

"We can kill ourselves."

Two minutes earlier she had been laughing because some men were jumping about, making fools of themselves. The change was so fantastic that I smiled. The smile was a mistake.

"Are you afraid?" Suddenly, she was breathing quickly and her eyes were gleaming with hatred. "It would be quite simple. We could jump from the terrace. It would be quick and not painful. But if you are afraid, I will do it myself."

She started up and I gripped her arm. "Rosalie, listen to me."

"What does it matter if a filthy Indo dies?" Then, she broke into Dutch and I could not understand much of what she said.

"Rosalie, listen!"

She hit me in the face and tried again to get away. I grabbed her arms, swung her round and forced her down on to the bed.

"For God's sake, stop it!" I said angrily.

She spat at me; then, for about a minute, she fought like a maniac; a maniac with closed eyes who cursed me savagely all the time in Dutch. When, at last, she went limp, I thought that she had fainted or that it was a trick to make me release my hold; but it was neither. After a moment, she caught her breath in a sob and began to cry helplessly. I took my hands away and sat down on the other bed to wait.

The leaflet lay crumpled on the bed beside me. After a bit, I picked it up and looked at it again. To me it had been no more than a smudgy proclamation of martial law; but to her it must have brought the smell of death. I tore it into small pieces, and wished that I could deal with my memory of the street-fighting sergeant in the same way.

She was quiet now. I fetched her a glass of water. She had pulled her hair down over her face so that I could not see her. When she had taken the glass from me, I turned away and began to pick up the fresh bits of plaster that had fallen from the ceiling.

The sounds of the battle had changed perceptibly. The attack was still coming from the west, but it had become possible to distinguish the firing of individual guns. At intervals there was the short, sharp crack of an eighty-eight. The destroyer was silent again. There was nothing new to be seen. Smoke from burning buildings had drifted across the whole area. I thought of the people in the crowded kampongs along the canal banks near the firing, and wondered what was happening to them. Were they swarming out, trying to get away towards the centre of the city, or were they huddled trembling inside their houses, waiting for the terror to pass them by? The latter, I hoped. The tanks and guns would stay on the metalled roads as much as they could, and the defenders would choose solid buildings from which to fight back rather than canal banks. Later, perhaps, when the defenders broke and the mopping-up process began, it might be wise to join in the killing and so demonstrate one's loyalty to the victors; but, for the present, it would be safer to remain passive.

I heard Rosalie put the empty glass down and move over to the mirror. I finished picking up the plaster and glanced at her. She was brushing her hair. She saw me in the mirror, looking at her, and stopped brushing. I went over to her and put my hands on her shoulders. She turned to face me.

"You do not dislike me now?"

"No."

"You are not pretending because you feel sorry for me?"

"No."

"If you were angry and beat me for what I said, I should feel more certain."

"Most of what you said I didn't understand."

"It was not polite."

"I know. There was something about my skin."

She flushed. "You understood that? I am sorry. I said it to humiliate myself."

"Does a European skin disgust you?"

"Sometimes." She looked up at me defiantly. "You see, I do not pretend with you. And sometimes, my own skin disgusts me because it is so dark. My father's was light, much lighter than yours. You are nearly as brown as I am. I like to touch and smell your body and to feel the strength of it. I do not think: 'He is a European, I am an Indo.' I think: 'It is good to be a woman with this man.'" She paused. "But sometimes it is different. You know how these men here can feel about me. That is how I can feel about myself. Part of me is European. Sometimes I hate it and want to kill it."

"What made you feel like that just now? Was it the leaflets? They don't really alter anything, you know."

165

"Perhaps not. I do not know. But I laughed at those officers dancing about like little boys when someone is throwing them coins, and forgot to be frightened. Then, when you showed me what was on the paper, it was worse than it had been before. It was like waiting for the *pemoedas* to come, and I wanted us both to die." She looked at me anxiously. "Do you understand?"

"Not altogether. Perhaps you have to be an Indo to understand completely."

She nodded. "Yes, perhaps you do." She hesitated. "It is curious to hear you use that word."

"You used it."

"And you do not dislike me for what I said?"

"No."

"Put your arms round me."

A few minutes later she said: "I do not really mind if I have to die, but I am afraid of being hurt."

"I know. So am I. The men in the next room are. The men firing those guns are. Everyone is—Indos, Sundanese, Europeans—everyone. There's nothing special about you."

"That is not polite."

"I don't have to be polite to you. It was part of the arrangement."

She smiled then. "You remember? That is very businesslike."

"Certainly. And dying was no part of the arrangement. If one of us is to be killed or wounded because we

166

happen to be here, that is another matter, but we are not going to kill ourselves."

"It is not much to kill oneself." She was still smiling.

"It is to me. Whatever happens, don't get that idea again, will you?"

Her smile faded and she looked up at me curiously. "Does it truly matter to you?"

"Yes, it matters."

After a moment she nodded. "Then as long as you are here, I will not think of it." She gathered up her hair and began to twist it into a bun on top of her head. "There is still water left in the bathhouse," she remarked; "perhaps we should use it while we can."

It was such a determined change of subject that it made me laugh.

She raised her eyebrows. "It will not be amusing if we cannot wash."

"You're right. It won't."

"Do you wish to go first?" She was still uneasy because I had laughed at her.

"No, you go ahead. If you use too much water, I shall beat you."

She smiled. I had made a feeble joke and she had regained face. All was well.

"May I wear your bathrobe?"

"Of course."

When she had gone, I ate a slice of papaya, lit a cigarette and went out on to the terrace. The bow-

167

legged officer was standing at the far end, looking out gloomily at the smoke haze. He nodded curtly when he caught sight of me, and I nodded back. We did not speak.

The firing had slackened off considerably and there were only occasional flurries of activity. It was as if both sides were weary of the argument, but could not quite make up their minds to abandon it. I found that a comforting notion. Unfortunately, I could not altogether conceal from myself the fact that what sounds there were seemed to come from very much nearer than they had an hour earlier.

Down in the leaflet-strewn square there was feverish activity. Fox-holes were being dug and the two-pounders were being manoeuvred into sandbagged pits so that they could cover the two western approaches to the square. One of the bomb craters was being used as a headquarters, another as an ammunition dump. Sounds from the Ministry of Public Health next door suggested that it, too, was being placed in a state of defence. Immediately below, beside the crater that had flooded the generator room, some men were unloading three-inch mortars from a truck. There were other men sitting on the ground fusing grenades. As far as I could see, there was only one small group of men in the entire square to whom a tank commander would have given a second thought. They were squatting under the trees, placidly scooping rice out of their bowls with their fingers. Laid out neatly on a groundsheet beside them were two American bazookas.

Someone came into the living room. Out of the corner of my eye, I saw the bow-legged officer turn and then go in quickly. A moment later I recognised Suparto's voice. There was a lot of firing going on just then and a truck down in the street below was spitting and back-firing as the driver revved it up, so I went back into the bedroom to see if I could hear what he was saying through the door.

It was not much better there. I could tell by the tone of his voice that he was giving orders, but that was all. Then, there was a pause, and I heard steps on the terrace. I had just time to move away from the door before Suparto came in by the window.

He nodded to me and glanced quickly round the room.

"She's bathing," I said.

He nodded. "That is as well. I have not much time and what I have to say is private."

"You might be heard in the next room."

"For the present, there is no one in the next room. Sanusi is shortly transferring his headquarters there." He sat down wearily and stretched his legs. His cheekbones stood out sharply and his skin was the colour of parchment. I realised that it was probably three days

since he had slept. His uniform, however, was as neat as
ever.

"May I know what's happening out there?"

"There will be an official statement issued at the
first opportunity. Colonel Roda is writing it at this very
moment."

"No jokes, Major, please."

He smiled. "My apologies. I was indulging myself.
The thought of Colonel Roda, whom I greatly dislike,
trying bravely to misrepresent a situation which is already hopeless is very enjoyable."

"Are you sure there's nobody in there who can hear
you?"

"I can see that you are nervous this morning, Mr.
Fraser."

"Yes."

"Well, I admit that this waiting is disagreeable. As
far as I know, the present situation is this. General
Ishak's troops broke through the outer defence positions without difficulty. Some rebel troops, however,
were commanded with more skill than he expected. Instead of waiting to be swallowed up, they moved. As a
result, General Ishak's teeth met on nothing, and he
will have to take another bite."

"You said that the situation was already hopeless."

"It is. The rebels have postponed defeat by a few
hours, that is all. They cannot get out now."

"Does General Sanusi know that?"

"Not yet." He paused. "That is what I wanted to tell you about, Mr. Fraser. During the next few hours Sanusi is going to discover some very disagreeable facts, and there is going to be a moment when he realises what has happened. He is a misguided man, but not a fool. He will look at the faces of those about him and wonder whom he has to thank for his defeat. He will think back over the past two years and try to remember all that has been said and done, and relate it to the present situation. You understand?"

"Yes, I do."

"He is not, as I have said, a fool, and it may be that he will come to a correct conclusion. If he does and I am there, he will be looking into my face. In that case, I have no doubt that I could kill him before he killed me, but I would certainly be killed myself a moment later. Do you still understand?"

"I think so. You've done your job. You're getting out."

He eyed me carefully. For the first time, I felt sorry for him. He was a brave man who had taken nerve-racking risks to serve his country's government; and although I knew nothing of his motives, I found it hard to believe that personal ambition figured very prominently among them. It was even possible that he was a patriot. But patriot or no, he was not sufficiently insensitive to enjoy that moment of success. It was understandable that he should suspect me of irony.

171

"You do not seem surprised, Mr. Fraser."

"Why should I be? You've been risking your life because you felt it necessary. Why go on doing so when the need no longer exists?"

"These things cannot always be decided so logically. I ask you to believe me when I say that treachery does not come naturally to me."

"I'm sure it doesn't. I said that you were a humane man. But, forgive my asking, why did you take this risk? Supposing Sanusi had succeeded. Would it have been such a disaster? The present Government may have your loyalty, but I cannot believe that it has your approval."

"Approval? Mr. Fraser, I dislike the Nasjah gang quite as much as I dislike Colonel Roda. Sanusi is right about some things. We did not win our independence from the Dutch. Force of circumstances delivered it into hands which were unfit to receive it. But we do not have hands that *are* fit. Revolution is therefore pointless. What this nation must have is time to learn about government. Meanwhile, we must choose between evils. The Nasjah Government is corrupt and incompetent, and foreigners laugh at us for it. But you have heard Sanusi. He is not himself an evil man. As a commander in the field he is excellent. As a Minister of Propaganda he might perform useful service. But what has he to offer as the leader of the nation? More mosques in Selampang? Excellent. But what else? Only the discipline of men like Roda, men hungry for power. I prefer the Nasjah gang. They are weak, but with them, at least, the machinery of representative government is preserved and gradual change is possible. In the end, if the Americans and you British do not interfere, there will be fresh, healthy growth. But we must have time and patience."

"It may not be the Americans and British who do the interfering."

"Communism? That is your bad dream, not ours. Ah yes, I know. You see the propaganda in the kampongs. But that is all you see, and all there is. If I could believe that among all the ordinary people of Sunda there were enough able and determined men to create one effective district political organisation of any kind, I should be happy."

"Then I wish you luck, Major. How are you going?"

He stood up. "I shall decide to make a reconnaissance of the situation in the city. Sanusi's troops are falling back to the centre here and there is a certain amount of confusion. It will not be difficult to walk through their lines. And I am expected."

"I see. It's good of you to come and tell me."

"That was not the only reason I came. Of course, I shall inform the commander of the assaulting forces of your detention here, so that the troops may be warned that you are friendly."

"Thank you."

173

He looked embarrassed. "I cannot promise that it will help you."

"No, I understand."

"Also, I had some advice to offer you. This building will probably be shelled. Our naval gunners are not highly skilled, but it is possible that they will score some hits. Unless you are forced to do so, however, do not move down from this floor. You will be safer here in the end. I need not tell you to keep out of Roda's way if you can. Desperate men are always dangerous."

"Yes."

"Have you enough food and water in here?"

"Enough for how long?"

"Until tonight."

"We could do with some more drinking-water, I think."

"Come with me."

I followed him out on to the terrace and through the empty living room to the kitchen.

There were three bottles of water left in the refrigerator.

"Will one bottle be sufficient?"

"I think so."

"Good. One other thing. It will be better if you dress as a European."

"I've kept some clean clothes specially for the occasion, Major. But it's a hot day. Do you think I need to wear a tie?"

He gave me a wintry smile. "A sense of humour is an excellent thing at times like these. It helps a man to be philosophical." There were voices along the corridor outside. "Go back now, Mr. Fraser," he added, and then turned and walked out quickly. As I went back through the living room, I could hear his voice in the corridor. "Everything is prepared, *Boeng*. Shall I give orders for coffee to be sent to you?"

Rosalie had just returned. She had heard us talking in the kitchen and was eager to know what was going on.

I told her briefly most of what I had learned.

"And it will be ended by tonight?" she asked.

"Apparently."

We looked at one another in silence for a moment; then she drew a deep breath and nodded.

"So."

"Yes." I picked up my towel. "I think that it's about time I went and shaved."

8

The shelling of the area around the Van Riebeeck Square began at one o'clock.

For three hours before that, insurgent troops had been straggling back from the forward positions and occupying the block of buildings which included the Air House and the Ministry of Public Health. On my way back from the bathhouse, I had looked over the balustrade and seen two more two-pounders being manhandled through the big doorway of the Air Terminal offices below, and a truck full of wounded being driven in the direction of the Telegraf Road. The only civilians to be seen were children. Some of them stood in awe-struck silence, watching the troops; others, bolder, were playing a war game round a bomb crater and jumping in and out of the fox-holes.

A little after eleven, there were several violent outbursts of firing. They seemed to come from about a mile away to the north. Immediately after the first one, the telephone in the next room began to ring. During the half-hour that followed, there was scarcely a moment when Sanusi or Roda was not on the telephone; but for most of the time there was such a lot of noise going on outside that, although I could distinguish odd words and sentences, I could not make sense of what was being said. Eventually, Sanusi and Roda went out on to the terrace, and there was a muttered conference over a map. If the bad news was beginning to filter through to them, they clearly did not want their staff inside the room to know too much about it. In the middle of the conference, Roda was called in to the telephone again; but Sanusi remained on the terrace, fidgeting uneasily with the map and staring down into the square. After a minute or two, Roda came back and there was another furtive discussion. Some decision seemed to come out of it, for in the end Sanusi nodded, and the two men turned and walked back inside. A few minutes later the radio was switched on, and I guessed that the staff had been left to their own devices.

The official communiqué was being broadcast at intervals of fifteen minutes, and part of it was similar enough to the one I had invented earlier that morning to make us both laugh. The rest was not so amusing, however. Six persons attempting to obstruct the movements of the National Freedom Army had been shot; twenty others had been arrested on suspicion of sabotage, and were being questioned. There was a warning that persons failing to obey orders promptly, or displaying reluctance to assist the National Freedom Army in its fight against the colonialist reactionaries who were attempting to defeat the will of the people, would be liable to summary trial and imprisonment with forfeiture of all property.

Rosalie began to worry about her sister and Mina. The fighting seemed to be moving towards the quarter in which they lived, and she was afraid that, in trying to get away from it, they would run into worse trouble when the Government forces began to close in from the east. We talked about it for some time, but I made no effort to reassure her; not merely because I knew that my reassurances would be worthless, but because I hoped that the more she worried about Mina and her sister, the less she would worry about herself.

A little after mid-day there were two extra-violent explosions that brought down some more fragments of plaster, and a few moments later we saw two columns of smoke mushrooming up over the warehouses in the direction of the old town. Rosalie said that one of the oil companies had their gasoline storage tanks in that area, but the smoke looked to me more like the result of demolition charges. I thought it probable that the defenders were now trying to delay the Government's encircling movements by blowing up canal bridges, and wondered if they yet knew that there were enemies, not friends, waiting across the line of their retreat.

I did not have to wait long for the answer. During the morning I had found a pack of cards in a drawer of Jebb's belongings, and at intervals since then I had been teaching Rosalie to play gin rummy. We had just sat down to resume our interrupted game when there was a sound of movement from the next room and the radio was switched off. Sanusi and Roda had returned.

For a few minutes, there was a steady murmur of voices punctuated by sharp monosyllables from Roda. Suddenly, chairs grated on the tiled floor and a door closed. Then, footsteps sounded on the terrace, the curtain was pushed aside, and the staff captain whom I had seen the previous day on the floor below peered in at us.

I looked up, and he beckoned.

"You, come."

"Where to?"

"See *Boeng*."

My heart was beating too insistently for comfort; but, for Rosalie's benefit, I put my cards down with a sigh of irritation and a word of apology before I stood up.

"You, come." He was belligerent now.

"I am coming."

I walked out on to the terrace and, with his hand on his pistol, he stood aside to let me pass. I took no notice of him and walked along to the living-room windows. There was no glass in them and I could clearly see the four men inside. Apart from Sanusi and Roda, there were a major and a lieutenant-colonel, both of them grey with dust and wearing steel helmets.

As before, it was Roda who took the initiative. He beckoned me in. The captain followed and stood behind me. Sanusi was sitting on the side of one of the long chairs, staring at the floor. He took no notice of me.

Roda glanced at the other two. "It was this *tuan* who repaired the radio power generator when a bomb damaged it yesterday. He is an engineer from Tangga."

The lieutenant-colonel nodded absently. The major stared. Sweat had caked the dust on their faces and their eyes were swollen with fatigue.

Roda stood up. "Mr. Fraser, you will answer some questions. Some of the answers we already have, so that we shall know whether you tell the truth or not. So, be careful."

I said nothing and waited.

"Have you seen Major Suparto today?"

"Certainly I've seen him."

"When?"

"I think it was shortly before the General and you came up here, nearly an hour after the planes came over that dropped leaflets."

"Where did you see him?"

"Here, naturally."

"What was said?"

"He told me that the General was returning to this

apartment, and that I should respect his desire for privacy by keeping off the terrace outside."

"What else?"

"He allowed me to fetch some drinking-water from the kitchen."

"What else?"

"Nothing more, I think. Oh yes, he mentioned that he was going to make a reconnaissance in the city."

Roda laughed shortly. Inside the room there was a silence. Not very far off, an eighty-eight was slamming away like a pair of double doors in a gale.

Sanusi raised his head. "Was nothing else said, Mr. Fraser?"

"No, General."

"Why should he tell you where he was going?"

"I've no idea, General."

"You knew Major Suparto when he was at Tangga. Were you friendly with him there?"

"Not particularly. He was employed by the contractors as a liaison manager. His duties were very different from mine."

"What was the opinion of Major Suparto at Tangga?"

"Very high. In fact . . ." I broke off.

"Go on, Mr. Fraser. Say what there is to be said."

"I was only going to say that Major Suparto was exceptional. The Government sent quite a lot of unemployed officers to work with us there. Major Suparto was the only one of them who had any real ability."

There was another brief silence. Sanusi looked at Roda. Roda stared back at him bitterly for a moment and then swung round to face the other two.

"You hear?" he said in Malay. "You remember the meeting at Kail? I asked then. Why should they send him to Tangga where it was so easy for him to contact us? Luck, you all said. Luck, and more. It showed that they did not have the smallest suspicion that he was one of us." He glared round the room. "Well, now you know better. Now you know . . ."

"That is enough," Sanusi broke in impatiently. "Many mistakes have been made. I did not believe that we were ready. I was for waiting another year, for letting them destroy themselves before we moved. I yielded to the Committee's judgment."

"A judgment based on information supplied by a traitor, *Boeng*."

"I am not reproaching you. We are men, not gods, Ahmad. We cannot read souls." Sanusi stood up and walked over to the table.

Perhaps because they were now speaking Malay they thought I did not understand. Perhaps they had forgotten me. I just stood there. They watched him as if they were waiting for an oracle, while he smoothed out a map and bent over it.

"Here are the possibilities," he said at last. "We can try to break out of the city and regain our base."

182

Roda shrugged. "That is their greatest hope, that we will try," he said.

Sanusi eyed him coldly. "We will consider all the possibilities, Ahmad. Your advice will be asked later. The second possibility is that we attempt to hold the centre of the city." He paused and this time Roda was silent. "The third possibility is that we negotiate with them." He looked at the lieutenant-colonel. "Well, Aroff? Your opinions?"

Aroff wiped his forehead with the back of his hand. "As to the first possibility, *Boeng,* I agree with Ahmad." He spoke huskily and kept clearing his throat. "As to the second, I have no objection to dying. As to the third, I do not understand how we can negotiate any-thing except surrender, and for us that only means dy-ing in a different way. I say that it is better to die like men than to die shamefully in a prison yard."

"Major Dahman?"

"I say the same, *Boeng.*"

"Ahmad?"

Roda stared round at them belligerently. "Are we whipped dogs? What is all this talk of dying?"

Aroff stiffened. "Can you give us guns, Ahmad?" he snapped. "Can you give us tanks? Can you, at this late hour, persuade the men who were to have fought with us to desert General Ishak? If so, we will talk of living."

"We are not whipped dogs," Sanusi interposed;

"and neither are we children. What is your opinion, Ahmad?"

"We should negotiate, *Boeng.* Consider. We are in a strong position here. They have tanks, yes, and they have guns, but they cannot stand at a distance and kill us all with high explosive. At Cassino, a few Germans held an army corps. At Stalingrad, it was the Germans who broke, not the Russkis. Ah yes, I know it is different with us. We are cut off from our supplies. Our ammunition will not last for ever. But if they want to kill us they will have to assault us, and that will be an expensive operation for them. They will prefer to negotiate."

"For our surrender, certainly they will negotiate," retorted Aroff; "but what terms can we expect?"

"An amnesty within two years. The terms to be witnessed by a neutral observer, the Indonesian Ambassador perhaps."

"They would be fools to agree."

"Why? We have a following in the country. They will not make themselves secure by killing us. Besides, think of the good impression it would create abroad."

Aroff turned protestingly to Sanusi. *"Boeng,* this is madness."

Sanusi started to say something and so did Roda. At the same instant, there was a quick rushing sound. Then, the floor jumped, a blast wave that felt like a sandbag clouted me in the chest and my head jarred to the whiplash violence of exploding T.N.T.

For a second I stood there, stupidly staring at the other men in the room who were staring stupidly at me. Then, I turned and blundered out on to the terrace. The shell had burst against a window embrasure on the floor below, and fumes and smoke were pouring up over the balustrade. As I began to cough, the staff captain pushed past me with an angry exclamation that I was too deafened to hear, and went to look down over the balustrade. Then, the fumes got him, too, and he turned away. I looked back into the room. Roda was holding the back of his hand against his forehead as if he were dazed. Sanusi was shouting something at him. I stumbled along the terrace to the bedroom.

Rosalie was sitting on my bed with her hands over her face, trembling violently. I was not feeling too good myself. If that was a sample of the shooting we could expect from the naval gunners, we were not going to last very long.

I put my arms round her and she looked up at me. The whistle of the second shell rose to a climax and we both ducked involuntarily. The burst that followed made a glass on the table tinkle against the water bottle standing beside it, but that was all. It was about three hundred yards over.

I produced the old platitude: "If you can hear it coming it's going to miss you."

It has never yet comforted anyone who was badly frightened, and it did not comfort her. The destroyer was firing its four guns singly, so that the bombardment was reasonably steady, but I soon realised that the first hit had been a fluke. When, after twenty minutes, the first burst of firing ceased, they had not succeeded in dropping another shell within fifty yards of the Air House. Perhaps they were not trying for it. For Rosalie, however, every round was aimed, not merely at the building we were in, but at our room in it. I moved one of the beds around so as to give us some protection from a burst on the terrace, and we lay down on the floor behind it, but I don't think she felt any more protected.

When the lull came, however, I made her go out on to the terrace with me to see what damage had been done. There were some craters in the square, and a small building on the far side was on fire; but that was about all that was visible. In fact, the closely built-up area behind us had taken the brunt of the shelling; but there was no point in telling her that. The damage to our own building was also out of sight. As she had clearly expected to find the entire square in ruins, all this produced a very satisfactory sense of anti-climax. We kept to the bathouse end of the terrace, and saw nothing of the men in the living room. I guessed that the council of war had been resumed on the other side of the building. Rosalie had heard something of what had been said while I was there, and now I told her the rest. The possibility of negotiation cheered her up considerably. I did not say what I thought of it. When we went back into the bedroom, I was able to persuade her to eat some fruit and begin another game of gin.

It was just after three when the staff captain came for me again.

Since two, the sounds of street-fighting had steadily been getting nearer, and we had had another twenty-minute bombardment from the destroyer. This had been both worse and better than the first; worse, because the gunners had dropped the range slightly and managed to put every shell into or around the square itself; better, because Rosalie, having decided that her earlier fears had been quite groundless, proposed that we should continue our game of gin on the floor. Admittedly, it was my hands that shook now, not hers, and she who was concerned on my account when a near miss made me fumble and scatter my cards; but on the whole it was an improvement on the earlier situation.

The staff captain was more polite this time. It was Colonel Roda who wished to see me, he explained; but why, he did not know. The radio in the next room was silent, and, with a sinking heart, I wondered if the generator had broken down again. The staff captain shrugged when I suggested this; he knew nothing. I told Rosalie that if I were going to be away for any length of time, I would try to get a message to her, and then went off with him.

He led me to an office on the third floor at the back of the building. The shell that had burst on the fifth floor had gutted three offices and brought down part of the wall along the corridor, but there had been no casualties, and no structural damage of any consequence. It had short-circuited the lights, however, and Alwi was along there trying to rectify the trouble. I asked him about the generator, but he said that it was running perfectly. By the time I reached Colonel Roda's office, I was both puzzled and worried.

The office into which the staff captain ushered me had the look of a board room after a directors' meeting. The air was full of tobacco smoke, and there was a litter of dirty coffee cups and crumpled scribbling paper. There had been seven men in there, but now there were only two: Roda and Aroff. The latter had cleaned himself up and wore a black cap in place of the steel helmet; but he looked even wearier than before. Roda's face was the colour of putty. It did not seem to have been a very successful meeting.

They were sitting at one end of the table reading through a document and comparing it with what was evidently the draft from which it had been typed. To my surprise, Roda waved me to a chair. I sat down as far away from them as possible and waited. When they had finished, Roda looked at Aroff inquiringly. Aroff nodded, but with the air of a man agreeing to something against his better judgment. Roda pursed his lips and turned to me.

"Mr. Fraser, we have sent for you because we believe that you may be willing to assist us."

"Oh yes?"

"The General and I were much impressed by your co-operation in the matter of the generator. Under circumstances of the greatest difficulty, without proper assistance or equipment, you employed your skill and knowledge to such good effect that the enemy's attempts to silence Radio Sunda were totally defeated." He smiled.

This was fantastic. For one wild moment I thought that he was about to pin a decoration on me: the Order of *Boeng* Sanusi (2nd Class) perhaps. I smiled back guardedly. Aroff, I noticed, was absently studying his fingernails, as if none of what was being said were any business of his.

"That being so," Roda continued amiably, "we do not think it unreasonable to assume that, as a British friend of Sunda, you are sympathetic to the policy and aspirations of the National Freedom Party and its leader."

I could have thought of several brief replies to that, but by now I was curious to know what he wanted.

I shook my head doubtfully. "As a foreigner, of course, it would be a gross impertinence for me to express an opinion about a political matter."

"Nevertheless, Mr. Fraser, we feel that you are not unsympathetic to the principles for which we stand. It is for that reason that we propose to take you into our confidence."

"I see." I did not see, but he evidently expected me to say something.

"Good. As you know, the Nasjah forces have counter-

189

attacked. At this moment a battle is being fought in the streets of our city. Now, I must tell you, Mr. Fraser, that but for the activities of certain enemy agents and the unconstitutional action of the Nasjah gang in arresting many of our supporters on false charges, this battle would not be going on. We should be in complete control. As it is, Sunda is faced not merely by civil war, but also by the devastation of large areas of our capital. Mr. Fraser, we are patriots, not savages. Sunda cannot tolerate civil war. Selampang cannot be permitted to suffer needlessly. General Sanusi has, therefore, taken the initiative in proposing to General Ishak, as between equals, an armistice, during which negotiations can take place for the evacuation of all armed forces from the city and the setting up of a joint commission of conciliation under neutral supervision."

It was not a bad bluff. If I had not talked to Suparto I might have swallowed it for a while. I glanced at Aroff. He had a knife out and was cleaning his fingernails now. I looked back at Roda.

"I wish you every success, Colonel. But I don't see how I can help you."

"I will explain, Mr. Fraser. We have been in telephone communication with General Ishak's headquarters and certain conditions have been agreed for a preliminary meeting to discuss the terms of the cease-fire. That meeting will take place, under flags of truce, in front of the police barracks at four o'clock. That is in half an hour." He paused and stirred uncomfortably.

"Yes, Colonel?"

"We asked that independent foreign observers should be present, so that any promises made or undertakings given should be properly witnessed. Consular or diplomatic representatives would have been suitable, but this was not agreed. The enemy refuse to permit accredited representatives of foreign powers to participate in what they say is a domestic political matter. They pretend that it would be contrary to protocol and an encroachment on our national sovereignty. In fact, of course, they are afraid to lose face. It has been agreed, however, that two foreign observers not of diplomatic status may attend, one for each side, providing that neither is a newspaper representative and neither of Dutch nationality. We would like you to attend for us, Mr. Fraser."

"Me? Why me? Surely there is someone more suitable in the area you control, some business man who fulfils the agreed conditions."

"There may be, Mr. Fraser, but we do not know where to find him at this moment. There is not much time."

"Frankly, I don't see why you need anyone at all." This was pure malice. I did see. Having nothing whatsoever to offer in exchange for the terms he was asking, and merely hoping to pull off a bluff, he was doing his best to make the negotiations seem formal and portentous. If the other side were the slightest bit unsure of themselves, it was just possible, too, that the presence of neutral observers might influence their judgment.

"The procedure has been agreed," he said coldly. He was tired of persuasion, and the fact that he would sooner be cutting my throat than asking for my co-operation was beginning to show in his eyes.

"Very well. What do I do?"

"Colonel Aroff will be our delegate. You will accompany him."

"What are my duties?"

"Firstly, to take note of what is said." He hesitated. "Should you feel, of course, that the other side are not viewing the situation correctly, you would be entitled to consult with their observer, and perhaps to protest." His eyes held mine. "I am sure you realise, Mr. Fraser, that it is in everyone's interest that an acceptable agreement is reached."

There was sufficient emphasis on the word "everyone." I understood now.

"May I know what terms you would accept?"

"Colonel Aroff has his instructions. He will explain them to you on the way. You should be leaving now."

Colonel Aroff put his knife away, stuffed the document they had been studying into his pocket and stood up. Then, with a nod to me he walked out of the room. He did not even look at Roda.

The staff captain was waiting in the corridor and,

as I followed Aroff out, he joined the procession. I noticed that he was carrying something that looked like a long cardboard tube in his hand. We followed Aroff down the stairs to the sandbagged entrance. There was a guard there who demanded passes before we were allowed to leave the building; Suparto having got away, the stable door was now bolted. The staff captain had the passes and we went through.

Outside in the road there was a jeep waiting which I recognised as the one from Tangga that Suparto had used. There was a soldier sitting in the driving seat. Aroff stopped and looked at the tube the staff captain was holding.

"Is that the flag of truce?"

"Yes, Colonel *tuan.*"

"It must not be shown here. Can you drive?"

"No, Colonel *tuan.*"

Aroff looked non-plussed. "Neither can I."

"I'll drive if you like, Colonel."

For the first time he looked at me directly. After a moment's thought, he nodded. "Good." He told the staff captain to go and dismiss the driver. "When men see a flag of truce," he added to me, "they begin to think of safety. After that it is hard to make them fight. The driver would have come back here and told them."

As we walked towards the jeep, a shell from the destroyer burst among the trees across the square and sent a lot of torn-off branches spurting up into the air. Another bombardment had begun. I remembered that I had not tried to send a message to Rosalie; but it was too late to do anything about that now. Another shell landed near one of the gun positions. As my ears returned to normal, I could hear a wounded man screaming.

"A waste of ammunition," Aroff remarked dourly. "Nearly two hundred rounds and what have they done with them? Six men killed and twenty wounded. It is absurd."

Absurd or not, they had also made a mess of some of the buildings in and around the square. One of the streets I tried to drive along was completely blocked by fallen rubble, and we had to make a detour. It was not easy. The area now being defended by Sanusi's troops was not much more than a quarter of a mile across in some places, and twice we had to reverse out of streets which had come under enemy fire. At several points, buses and trucks had been turned on to their sides and teams of civilians, women as well as men, were being forced by squads of troops to drag the vehicles broadside on to form tank obstacles. I saw no other civilians on the streets and the shops were all shuttered. Once, I caught a glimpse of a child's face at a window, but I was too busy driving to look about me much.

The police barracks were opposite the telephone

exchange in a long, straight road that began somewhere in the Chinese section and ended at the airport. About two hundred yards short of the barracks, we came to a canal crossing with a cinema on one corner and a barricade of overturned cars across the roadway. There was a two-pounder behind one of the cars, and in the deep storm drains on either side of the road a couple of machine-gunners. As I pulled up at the barricade, an officer who looked like a recently promoted N.C.O. moved out of a doorway and hurried over.

Aroff returned the man's salute casually.

"Have you been notified of the arrangements, Lieutenant?"

"Yes, Colonel *tuan*."

Aroff looked up at the bullet-scarred walls of the godown that stretched along one side of the road.

"You were under fire here until when?"

"Until ten minutes ago, Colonel *tuan*." He pointed with pride to the empty cases lying on the ground behind the two-pounder. "And they did not have it all their own way. The armoured car they sent did not like our gun."

"Did you destroy the armoured car?"

"Ah no, *tuan*." He smiled tolerantly, as if at a foolish question. "But they did not return for more. They have brought up a tank now."

"Where are the rest of your men?"

"On the roof of the godown, *tuan*."

Aroff looked at his watch. "We have five minutes, Mr. Fraser. We must discuss the situation."

He climbed out of the jeep, and I followed him as he walked over to the barricade. The staff captain seemed about to follow, then he thought better of it and began to talk to the lieutenant.

Aroff peered through the gap between two of the overturned cars which the gunners were using as an embrasure, and motioned to me to do the same. The crew squatting in the shade of one of the trucks looked up at us drowsily.

Except for a dead dog lying just beyond the canal, the road between the barricade and the police barracks was empty. The only visible sign of life in the ramshackle apartment houses which flanked it was a line of washing strung between two of the windows; but the sound of gunfire was comparatively distant now, and I could hear a man coughing in one of the houses. Outside the police barracks, in the centre of the road, and with its gun pointing directly at us, stood a medium tank.

Aroff was watching me as I straightened up.

"Are you a soldier, Mr. Fraser?"

"I was in the British army."

"An officer?"

"Yes, in the Engineers. Why?"

He drew me away and we walked back along the

road for a few yards. When we were out of earshot of
the gunners, he stopped.

"Should that tank you see there decide to move along
this road, Mr. Fraser, what do you think will happen?"

"How do you mean?"

"Do you see anything here to stop it?"

"Not a thing. The two-pounder's shot will bounce
off it. It'll just push this road block out of the way and
drive on. Unless, that is, you've got an anti-tank mine
under that crossing."

"We have no mines."

"And no other anti-tank weapons?"

"Here, none."

"Then there's nothing to stop it."

"Exactly." He produced the document from his
pocket, and held it out to me. "Do you wish to read
this?"

"I think Colonel Roda made its contents clear."

"Then we understand one another. All I have to
offer them, in fact, is a small saving of effort. The rest
is pretence, and, of course, they will know that."

"What do you want me to do, Colonel?"

He shrugged. "Is it of interest to you what happens
to us?"

"If there is any prospect of a cease-fire, naturally
I'll do everything I can to help."

"Then I will make only one request to you, Mr.
Fraser."

"Yes?"

"General Ishak is a military man. If you should have to refer to Roda, please do not call him Colonel Roda. In General Ishak's army he was a captain."

"And General Sanusi?"

"Colonel Sanusi would be more discreet."

"What about you, Colonel?"

He smiled slightly. "I received no promotion. But I do not think that General Ishak will regard that as a point in my favour. We shall, of course, speak Malay."

He looked at his watch again, then turned and walked towards the jeep.

The staff captain came forward and, when Aroff nodded, he took the white flag of truce out of its cardboard wrapping and fixed it on to the windscreen of the jeep.

I saw the gunners staring at it incredulously. Then, the lieutenant shouted an order and they scrambled to their feet. Another order, and they rolled the gun back clear of the barricade. The machine-gunners helped them to swing one of the cars aside a foot or two, so that there was space for the jeep to go through.

Aroff took no notice of these preparations. He had got into the jeep and was sitting there woodenly under the flag. I went and sat beside him in the driving seat while the staff captain clambered into the back. We sat there for a moment or two, then Aroff looked at his watch again and nodded to me.

I drove through the gap in the barricade on to the road ahead.

"Slowly, Mr. Fraser," Aroff said; "and keep to the centre."

I needed no telling. The moment we were clear of the barricade I felt horribly exposed; I was almost sure that the tank was going to open fire on us. The white flag drooping on its stick above us seemed a totally inadequate protection. It only wanted one trigger-happy idiot to start, I thought, and every gun in Selampang would be firing at us. I had no hat and was already far too warm. As I drove, sweat began to trickle into my eyes.

The first hundred yards was the worst. After that, although I could see the muzzle of the tank's gun dropping gradually as the gunner kept us in his sights, I knew that unless we suddenly drove straight at him brandishing anti-tank grenades, he was not going to fire. Also I could see a group of officers standing in the shade by the gate of the police barracks, waiting.

When we were within ten yards of the tank, a lieutenant in the Government uniform stepped out from behind it and held up his hand. I stopped with a jerk that made the staff captain lurch against the back of my seat.

Aroff got out stiffly and stood beside the jeep. When the staff captain and I had joined him, the lieutenant advanced and stopped in front of us.

"Follow me, please," he said curtly.

He turned then, and we followed him past the tank and over to the gateway. The group of officers was no longer there, only two sentries who stared at us curiously. The lieutenant led the way through into the courtyard of the barracks and the two sentries closed in behind us.

There was a big sago palm in the centre, and a table and chair had been placed in the shade of it. General Ishak sat at the table. Standing behind him were four officers and a civilian. I had never seen Ishak before. He was a thin, bitter-looking man with angry eyes and one of those wispy Sundanese moustaches that look as if they have just been stuck on with spirit gum. More interesting to me at that moment, however, was the fact that just behind him, still haggard but crisp and clean in his proper uniform, stood Major Suparto. As we came up to the table, I saw his eyes flicker towards me, but he gave no sign of recognition.

Aroff stopped and saluted the General.

Ishak did not return the salute. For a moment the two men stared at one another in silence. I was standing a little behind Aroff and I could see the muscles of his jaw twitching. Ishak looked at me.

"Who is this?" I recognised the voice. It was light and ugly, and sounded as if he were trying to speak and swallow at the same time. I had heard it once before that week.

"Mr. Fraser, an engineer from the Tangga Valley project, General. He is here by agreement as an observer."

"Very well." He glanced at the civilian who stood next to Suparto. "This is Mr. Petersen of the Malayan Rubber Agency."

"Dutch?" Aroff demanded sharply.

"Danish," said Mr. Petersen. He was a stout, fleshy-faced man in the late fifties, wearing a suit as well as a tie and looking as if he might at any moment collapse from the heat. I nodded to him and he smiled nervously.

Ishak yawned. "Although why foreign observers should be necessary to witness a simple police operation is not easy to understand," he said, and looked up at Aroff. "Well, this meeting is at Sanusi's request. He can only wish to surrender. It remains for me to inform you about the time and place. You agree?"

"No, General. All I am instructed to discuss are the terms of an armistice."

"What armistice? What terms?"

Aroff fumbled in his pocket and drew out the document. "I have the proposals here."

Ishak took the document, glanced through it impassively and then passed it to a colonel, presumably his chief of staff, who was standing behind him. Suparto read it over the colonel's shoulder. When they had finished, the colonel handed it back to Ishak. The latter glanced through it again and then looked at Aroff.

"Before you became a traitor, Aroff," he said, "you used to be an intelligent man." He tore the document in half and dropped the pieces on the table. "What has happened to you?"

"I am here to discuss terms, General." Aroff's voice was very carefully controlled.

Ishak flicked the torn paper away from him. "That discussion is ended. If you do not wish to make any personal explanation, then we will waste no more time. You may go."

Aroff did not move. "The document, General, was intended as a basis for negotiations. It can be modified."

Ishak shook his head. "It cannot be modified. You are not here to negotiate or to discuss terms. If you are not here to offer surrender, then we are wasting time." He stood up. "You have five minutes to get back to your lines."

Aroff hesitated, then he gave in. "On what terms would you accept a surrender, General?"

"I will tell you. Your masters say that they wish to avoid useless suffering and damage to property. So do I. On that point we agree. Very well. I will accept the surrender of all members of your rebel force who disarm themselves, form themselves into separate parties of not more than twenty-five, and march under flags of surrender to the square in front of the railroad station.

Each party should appoint a leader who will carry the white flag, and every man must bring any food he has with him. All arms and ammunition must be left behind under guard in the Van Riebeeck square until our troops arrive there."

"What treatment would those who surrender receive?"

"For the present they will be treated as if they were foreign prisoners of war under the terms of the Geneva Convention. Later, no doubt, after a year, perhaps, an amnesty will be granted. That is all, I think. Do those terms seem harsh to you, Aroff?"

Aroff shook his head.

Ishak smiled unpleasantly. "After what has happened, they seem to me absurdly lenient. Politicians' terms, Aroff! You should be laughing."

Aroff sighed. "You were good enough to say that I was an intelligent man, General. You would have more dignity if you treated me as one."

"What more do you want, Aroff? A free pardon?"

"The list of exceptions, General. The list of those whose surrender will not be accepted."

"Ah yes, the outlaws." He held out his hand and Suparto gave him a paper. "Let us see. Sanusi, Roda, Aroff, Dahman . . . I am sorry to tell you that you are on the list. Shall I read any more?"

"If Major Suparto drew it up, I am sure it is complete." Aroff looked straight at Suparto, and I was glad I could not see his eyes.

Suparto stared back impassively.

Ishak handed Aroff the paper. "Your masters will want to see that. They have half an hour in which to let us know that they accept our terms."

"Terms, General?" Aroff said bitterly. "You mean a death sentence, surely!"

"No, Aroff." Ishak's eyes narrowed. "That sentence has been passed already. It is no longer a question of whether you all die or not, but only of how you die and of how many of your men die with you. We shall see now what value your leader puts on his men's lives." He turned to Suparto. "Send them back."

Ishak began to walk towards the barrack entrance. Suparto moved after him quickly and said something. Ishak paused. I saw him glance back at me and then nod to Suparto before walking on.

Suparto came over to Aroff.

"Mr. Fraser is a foreigner and a non-combatant. Is it necessary for him to return with you?"

Aroff shrugged. "I don't know. I suppose not."

"It is very necessary," I said.

They both stared at me.

Suparto frowned. "Why?"

"Roda left me in no doubt that he regards Miss Linden as a hostage."

"That is absurd."

"It wasn't absurd yesterday, Major. You should know that."

"The situation is now different."

"Not for Miss Linden. She's still up there in that apartment. I'm very grateful to you for the suggestion, but I think I must go back."

He sighed irritably. "This is foolishness, Mr. Fraser. The woman is not your wife."

"Perhaps Mr. Fraser has scruples about betraying those who trust him," said Aroff.

Suparto stood absolutely still, his face a mask. For a moment he stared at Aroff, then he nodded to the lieutenant who was waiting to escort us back to the jeep.

Aroff was smiling as he turned away.

The jeep had been standing out in the sun and the metal on it was painful to touch. I made a clumsy job of turning it between the deep drains. My movements were hampered, too, by the staff captain, who was leaning forward across the back of my seat, pleading with Aroff.

"The list, Colonel. May I see the list?"

"Not now."

"A man has a right to know if he is to die."

"All men have to die, Captain."

"If I could see the list."

"Not while they are watching us. Have you no dignity?"

205

"For the love of Allah, tell me."

"Are you a renegade? Did you formerly hold a commission from the Republic?"

"You know that I did, Colonel."

"Then you will be on the list."

I managed to get the jeep round at last and drove back towards the barricade. Behind me, the staff captain began to weep.

From this side of the canal crossing I could see the front of the cinema. Above the portico there was a big advertising cut-out. Next week, it said, they would be showing *Samson and Delilah.*

When we arrived back at the square, the shelling had stopped. The Ministry of Public Health had had a direct hit on the roof, and smoke was drifting up from the smouldering débris below. Outside the Air House there was a pile of rubble that seemed to have fallen from one of the upper floors. All over the square there were men still digging in. There was an insistent racket of machine-gun fire. It seemed to be coming from somewhere only two or three streets away.

Rosalie had been alone for nearly an hour and I was worried about her. The only time Aroff had spoken since we had re-crossed the canal had been to tell m to stop so that the wretched staff captain could remove the flag of truce. When we left the jeep, I drew him aside.

"I don't think I can be much help to you with Roda, do you, Colonel?"

He thought for a moment and then he said: "No. This captain will escort you back. I will tell Roda that I ordered it."

"Is there any reason why Miss Linden and I should remain here?"

"None, except that you would need Roda's permission to leave. At this moment, it would not be wise to ask for it."

"I see what you mean."

"Besides, where would you go? The streets would be more dangerous for you than this place, and who would take you into his house at such a time?"

"Perhaps there will be a surrender?"

He shook his head. "They will never agree. They will dream of miraculous escapes. Ishak knows that. He is only humiliating us. He means to destroy us all."

"If it rested with you, Colonel, would you accept?"

He shrugged wearily. "If it had rested with me, I would never have attempted to negotiate. I am not so afraid of death. Now, we have lost face and will die ashamed." He hesitated and then gave me a little bow of dismissal. "Your company has been a pleasure, Mr. Fraser."

The staff captain left me at the door of the apartment and hurried back downstairs, presumably to make his own panic-stricken contribution to the discussion of Ishak's surrender terms.

The door from the hall into the living room was

shut. If there were any officers inside I did not want to walk in on them unexpectedly. I knocked. There was no reply; but as I opened the door I had a shock.

When I had left, the sun roof over the terrace had been propped up fairly securely, and the screens were in place. Now there was no sun roof and the screens were flattened. One of the long chairs was lying across the balustrade. I ran through on to the terrace.

The shell had landed on the terrace of one of the unfinished apartments about thirty feet beyond the barrier wall with the spikes on it, and had dislodged a whole section of the balustrade there. The barrier wall was sagging like an unhinged door, and the blast had lifted the roof off the bathhouse.

As I saw this and started towards the bedroom shouting for Rosalie, I stumbled over one of the screens. Then, I saw her running towards me along the terrace and went to meet her.

For a minute or so she clung to me, sobbing. It was only relief, she explained after a while; relief that I was back. She had really not been very frightened when the shell burst; it had been so sudden. It was right what I had told her about shells and the noise they made. She had not heard this one coming.

All this time she had been holding the water scoop from the bathhouse in her hand. Now, she explained that the cistern had collapsed into the bathhouse when the roof had lifted, and that she had been trying to transfer what was left of the water into the ewer before it all leaked away.

I went along there with her and had a look at the damage. If the cistern had been full it would have crashed through to the floor. As it was, the pipes had held it up, though one of them had fractured and was gradually draining it. I got a jug from the kitchen and between us we managed to get most of the water into the ewer. While we were doing this, I told her about the surrender offer and what Colonel Aroff had said.

She took the news calmly.

"General Ishak is a swine," was her comment.

"You know him?"

"Everyone knows about him. Mina has a very funny scandal. He sleeps with young men, you know. They say that even so he can do nothing. When you spoke to Major Suparto, did he say anything about us?"

"I only had a word or two with him."

"Do you think he will try to help us?"

"If he can, he will."

She fell silent. The cistern just above our heads was vibrating to the concussion of an eighty-eight which was slamming away somewhere along the Telegraf Road. I knew that she was listening to the noise carefully and beginning to wonder about the violence it represented. She had a standard of comparison now.

"I think it's time we had a drink," I said.

9

The first tank reached the Van Riebeeck Square just before sundown.

No great flights of military imagination had been needed to devise General Ishak's plan of attack. The modern dock area south of the river had been quietly occupied by Government troops after the bombing of the road and rail bridges the previous afternoon. It was only the semi-circle of city north of the river, and centred on the Van Riebeeck Square, that he had to take by force. The rebel outer defence ring had been held together by three strong points: the canal network of the old port, the garrison barracks and a rubber factory in the suburbs. He had decided to make his break-through a little to the south of the barracks under a covering bombardment from the destroyer, then fan out right and left, rolling up the outer defences as he went. Finally, he would turn east again and send three armoured columns to converge on rebel headquarters. In view of the superior forces at his disposal, there was no likelihood of the plan failing. All that remained to be learned was how soon it would succeed.

The reduction of the outer defences had been all but completed by mid-day, though it had not been quite as easy as Ishak had expected. At several points, the defenders had been agile enough to slip through his cumbersome enveloping movements and re-establish themselves in new positions; but in the end, they were squeezed back, and all they succeeded in gaining for themselves by their efforts was a little time that they could not use. By three o'clock the turn to the east had been made, and the armoured columns were carving their way through towards the centre, the speed of their advance controlled only by that of the infantry mopping up behind them.

Not long after five, there was a tremendous burst of firing along the Telegraf Road; machine guns, mortars, a two-pounder; the noise was deafening. The sun was low now, and I could see smoke drifting up over the roofs less than a quarter of a mile away. Where the Telegraf Road entered the square there was a sudden flurry of activity. There were men running back out of the road and other men running forward into it. Then, one of the two-pounders out in the square began to fire. I heard Rosalie give a startled gasp and turned round. She was crouching behind the balustrade with her fingers in her ears. When I looked back across the square, there were no running men. One of them was lying face downwards in the centre of the road. The rest had taken cover against the walls of the building that jutted out on the corner. The two-pounder was firing rapidly, bouncing about in its shallow pit, sending up a cloud of yellow dust and adding to the racket of the machine guns; then, for an instant, there was a gap in the sound, and through it I heard the shrill squeaking of a tank's tracks.

It nosed out of the end of the road, and seemed to hesitate there for a moment like a dull-witted bull blinking in the sunlight of the arena. There was a black stain down the side of it that looked as if it had been made by an oil bomb. The two-pounder fired twice and I saw a streak of silver appear on the turret. Every automatic weapon in the square seemed to be firing at that moment, and the sound of the tank's own machine gun was lost in the din. But it was the tank's gun that was effective. Dust spurted up all around the two-pounder, and suddenly it was no longer firing. I saw one of the gunners start to crawl out of the pit, and then a second burst finished him. Two more bursts wiped out the crews of two of the machine guns.

The tank lurched forward and then made a left turn. It controlled the square now, and was ready to demonstrate the fact to anyone foolish enough to dispute it. Apparently, nobody was. The crew of the other two-pounder out in the square were scrambling for cover among the trees, and the remaining machine-gunners who, a moment ago, had been blazing away so fiercely at the tank's armour plating, were now crouching discreetly in their fox-holes. The tank began to move along the north side of the square searching for targets. From away across the square some optimist began dropping mortar bombs near it. And then, suddenly the situation changed. There was a noise like an enormous paper bag being exploded. Immediately on top of it there was a spine-jarring crack. At the same moment the tank swung round broadside on and stopped in a cloud of dust.

The commander of it knew his job. Within a few seconds, he was putting down smoke; though not before another bazooka bomb had sent fragments of the broken track screaming up through the trees overhead. As the smoke drifted back across the tank, I could see the turret traversing rapidly and knew that the commander had spotted the bazookas' position. If the men handling them did not move quickly, they would become sitting targets as soon as the smoke thinned; but, like innocents, they were settling down expectantly to wait for another chance to knock the tank out.

Rosalie touched my arm. I looked round and saw that Roda had come into the living room. We went back quickly into the bedroom.

After a moment, Sanusi walked out on to the terrace

213

and looked down on to the square. Roda was talking to
someone in the next room, but it was impossible to
hear the conversation. When the other person went,
Roda joined Sanusi at the balustrade.

There was some sort of disagreement between the
two men. Roda was trying to persuade Sanusi of something and Sanusi would appear to be listening; then he
would turn away abruptly and Roda would have to go
after him and begin all over again. Once Sanusi turned
sharply and asked a question. Roda had his document
case with him, and in reply he held it up and patted it.

Down in the square, the tank's turret gun began
firing suddenly and the building shook as something
crashed into it. Rosalie looked at me inquiringly. I said
I thought that the tank was firing at the place where
the bazooka crews were dug in, and that the shot had
probably ricocheted into the building down below. She
nodded understandingly, as if I had been apologising
for the noise made by an inconsiderate neighbour.

Another tank had entered the square now. I could
hear it squeaking along the road in the opposite direction to the first one and firing bursts from its machine
gun.

Then, the sun went down, and for nearly a minute
there was no sound from the square except the squeaking of the tank tracks. Along the Telegraf Road, however, the firing intensified and I could hear the thump-

ing of grenades. The infantry were moving up now, clearing the defended houses that the tanks had left behind them. Now and again, the drifting smoke would be illuminated momentarily by the flash of an explosion below.

A shoe grated outside on the terrace.

"Mr. Fraser." It was Roda's voice.

I went to the window. There were no lights on in the apartment, nor was there a moon yet. He was about ten feet away and for a moment I did not see him.

"Yes, Colonel?"

"Come here, please."

I went over. Beyond him, along the terrace, Sanusi stirred and rested his elbows on the balustrade.

Roda lowered his voice. "I must speak in confidence to you, Mr. Fraser."

"Yes?"

"It has become necessary for the General and myself to leave this headquarters."

"Yes?"

"We have done all we can here. It is better to live for a cause than to die for it uselessly. That is our choice now. I have persuaded our *Boeng* that it is his duty to live."

"I see."

"It has been a difficult decision, you will understand." He paused.

215

"I can see that."

"More difficult than you might think."

"No doubt." I was trying unavailingly to understand the reason for these confidences.

"For two men, withdrawal from this headquarters is still possible. If more should attempt it, all will fail. There must be secrecy."

"Of course." That, at least, I could understand.

"As there was when Napoleon withdrew from Egypt."

For a moment, I thought that he was making a tasteless joke. But no; his lips were pursed solemnly. He saw himself as the Marmont of this occasion.

I mumbled agreement.

"I tell you this, Mr. Fraser, because there is a matter in which you can help us."

"Yes?"

"If we are to withdraw successfully we cannot go in our uniforms."

"I see that."

"It is the shirts. Our pants will attract no attention. We merely need civilian shirts. I think you have some."

"Shirts?" I stared at him stupidly.

"Two will be enough. You have clean ones?"

"Yes, I have." I also had a terrible desire to laugh.

"Then perhaps you will get them."

"Now?"

"At once, please."

I turned and went back into the bedroom. In there, I tried switching on the light, but the power was off. Rosalie watched me incredulously, while I struck a match and began fumbling in the drawers. I knew that I had only one clean shirt left. This round would have to be on Jebb. I found the right drawer eventually, picked out two of the oldest shirts there, and took them out on to the terrace. Roda nodded approval.

"I'm afraid they will be a bit large for you, Colonel."

"That is unimportant." He folded them carefully and put them in his document case. "They are light-coloured but not . . ."

"Colonel!" It was Sanusi's voice.

Roda turned inquiringly.

Sanusi had moved away from the balustrade and was standing in the centre of the terrace. I thought I saw a pistol in his hand, but it was too dark to see properly. At the same moment, there were footsteps in the living room, and Aroff and Major Dahman came out on to the terrace.

"*Boeng,*" Aroff began, "you sent for us?"

"Yes," said Sanusi; and then he fired.

The first bullet hit Roda in the stomach. For a second, he stood quite still; then he dropped the document case and took a step forward. The second bullet hit him in the right shoulder and he twisted forward on to his knees. He began to say something, but Sanusi paid no attention to him.

To Aroff and Dahman, he said: "I sent for you to witness an execution." Then, he went up to Roda and shot him again in the back of the head.

Roda slid forward on to his face.

Aroff and Dahman did not move as Sanusi turned towards them. Across the square, one of the tanks began firing its turret gun.

"What was the offence, *Boeng?*" Aroff said.

"He was attempting to desert. You will find the evidence in there." He shone a flashlight on to the document case. "Open it."

Aroff walked over to the document case and opened it up. The shirts fell out. He looked up at me.

"Yes, they were from the Englishman," said Sanusi. "I leave that matter to you. All officers of the defence force must be informed of the execution and the reason. The body should be put where they can see it. For the public I shall issue a simple statement informing them that, in view of the pressure of Colonel Roda's military duties, I have taken over the Secretaryship of the Party for the time being. There must be no suggestion at this moment of a division in our ranks. I also have to consider world opinion. Firmness in such matters is not always understood."

He made these announcements with the cool author-

ity of a leader secure in the possession of great power
and the habit of using it with wisdom and restraint. He
seemed totally unaware of their absurd incongruity. I
saw Aroff look at him sharply.

"We have yet to hear from Djakarta," Sanusi added;
"I think the time has come for me to speak to President
Soekarno personally." With a nod to Aroff, he turned
and walked away through the living room.

Aroff looked at Dahman, who shrugged slightly, and
then at me. "What happened, Mr. Fraser?"

I told him. He made no comment. When I had finished he looked at Dahman.

"Well, Major, what do you think?" He nodded towards Roda's body. "Perhaps he was right. Of two men,
one might be lucky."

Dahman smiled grimly. "And the other? I have seen
Ishak's way of putting a renegade to death. I would
prefer to shoot myself now rather than risk that."

"Are you a coward, Dahman?"

"About some things, Colonel."

"So am I." Aroff handed the shirts to me. "You see,
Mr. Fraser? We have no use for them either." A gun
flash lit up his face for an instant as he looked out
across the square. "They will have their artillery up
soon," he remarked; "then, there will be no more
doubts to trouble us."

He turned to leave but at the living-room window he

paused and looked back. "Mr. Fraser, if Roda had anything else belonging to you, something that you may need, you should take it at once."

I stood there staring after him uncertainly as he went through into the corridor. Then, Rosalie was at my elbow.

"Steven! He means the pistol."

"Are you sure?" I was still trying not to be sick.

"Yes. He means you to take the pistol."

"All right."

The holster was near enough to the side for me to get the pistol out of it without getting blood on my hands, but the spare magazines were on the other side of the belt, and I knew that I would have to turn the body over to get at them. There was a sound of footsteps in the corridor. We hurried back to the bedroom and I slipped the pistol into a drawer with the shirts on top of it.

The guards had a simple way of moving the body. They rolled it on to a mat that they had taken out of the living room and dragged it away. As they went, they made jokes about Roda's plumpness. They seemed in excellent spirits. In one respect, at least, Sanusi's officers had been successful; they had managed to conceal the truth about their predicament from the unfortunate rank and file.

When they had gone, I got a flashlight out of my suitcase and examined the pistol. It had a full magazine in it and there was a round in the breech. Rosalie watched intently, and when I had unloaded it to make sure that I knew how it worked, she asked if she might handle it.

The possession of the pistol obviously pleased her a great deal more than it pleased me. I remembered how, when I had wakened her the first night, thinking that there were thieves getting into the apartment, her first thought had been to ask if I had a revolver.

When I had shown her how to load and fire it and had explained the safety catch, I thought that I had better try to modify her enthusiasm for the thing.

"Pistols are not really very much use except for frightening people," I said.

"Colonel Roda would not agree with you."

"The General was six feet away and Roda wasn't expecting it. I've seen people miss a target in broad daylight with a pistol at that range."

"But if anyone attacks us, we can kill him."

"The fact that you have a pistol can be more dangerous than being unarmed. A soldier might not kill an unarmed civilian, but if he sees someone facing him with a gun in his hand, he may shoot rather than take a chance."

"I think it is better to have it."

"As long as we don't have to use it, it's fine."

"You had a revolver."

"There was a time up in Tangga when there were a

lot of snakes about, and sometimes they got into our rooms. So I had a revolver. But the only time I tried to use it I missed, and after that I kept a shot-gun. I left that behind."

"Then the pistol is no good?" She sounded bitterly disappointed.

"It's an excellent pistol, and, as you say, it's better to have it than not. But what we need at this moment is somewhere to go when the fighting starts."

"When it *starts?* What is all that going on over there?"

There was, indeed, a fierce machine-gun and mortar battle going on around the College of Agriculture on the far side of the square. Some of Sanusi's troops had dug themselves in in the College grounds, and now the Government infantry were having to ferret them out.

"When it starts here, I mean. It's not going to be easy for them to take this building. They'll have to do it floor by floor. I don't want to be here when they start throwing grenades about."

"But where is there to go?"

"The roof would be safer. It's not so enclosed. I want to try and find the way up there. Will you come with me or would you sooner stay here?"

"I will come with you."

I hung the pistol by its trigger guard on a nail at the back of the cupboard, and we went out on to the terrace.

A car outside the big building at the end of the Telegraf Road was on fire, and the immobilised tank was using armour-piercing shot to break up a sandbagged defence position in one of the corner shops. The smoke and the glare and the noise made it all seem like a sequence from a somewhat improbable war film. The glare, however, was useful.

We went along the terrace past the bathhouse to the barrier wall which had been dislocated by the shell burst. There was a gap between the wall and the balustrade, and it was not too difficult to squeeze through. Beyond it we had to walk carefully. This terrace did not broaden out as Jebb's did, and the rubble was piled up against the balustrade. Farther along, where the balustrade had broken away and fallen down into the roadway, it was impassable; but by going through what should have been the bed and living rooms, it was possible to get round on to the terrace again beyond the obstruction. No more barrier walls had yet been erected, and from there on it was easy. I knew that somewhere on that floor there must be a stairway up to the roof. What I had wanted to find was a way of getting to it without being seen or having to pass the sentry stationed outside the apartment. By going along the terraces of the unfinished apartments for most of the way, it was possible to reach the stairway without using any of the passage visible to the sentry.

The roof was quite flat with an eighteen-inch parapet running round it. At intervals along the parapet concrete blocks had been let in to hold the guy wires for the radio masts. There were the usual water tanks and ventilating shafts.

The sounds of the battle for the College of Agriculture had died down, and we had just started to walk over to the parapet, when there was a bright flash from somewhere way across the square, a stab of pain in my ears and the whole building jumped as if it had been dynamited. For one absurd instant, I even thought that it had. Then there was another flash, and the same thing happened again. General Ishak had brought his guns into action.

We hurried down the stairs and back to the apartment. There was no point in hurrying: I suppose that it was just a panic desire to be in familiar surroundings. As we went along one of the terraces, I could see that there were two more tanks in the square now, and that they were moving round the perimeter into positions from which they could give covering fire to the assault troops. The eighty-eights were firing at twenty-second intervals and with shattering effect. At that range they could not miss. When the first rounds had landed there had been shouts and screams from below. Now, those had stopped. After about five minutes the guns changed their targets. One of them began to take pot shots at the first-floor windows. The others started to pound the Ministry of Public Health.

There was nobody in the apartment when we returned, but I guessed that it would not be long before a general movement away from the lower floors began. I told Rosalie to put anything of special value that she had there into her handbag. My money and air ticket, and the few personal papers that I had, I stuffed into my pockets. Then, I took the pistol and a bottle of water and hid them along the terrace where they could be picked up easily when we moved out.

The din was appalling now and the whole place shook continually. Rosalie seemed more bewildered by the noise than frightened. When she had collected what she wanted to take with her and I gave her a glass of whisky, it was my hand that was shaking. I had made up my mind that the moment to move would be when the assault began. From then on, there would be little chance of anyone caring where we were; it would be everyone for himself. The trouble with me was that I could no longer see what was going on. Once or twice, a machine gun in the square had sprayed the windows of the floor below with bullets, and I knew that if I tried looking over the balustrade now I should almost certainly be seen and draw fire. So I had to sit there drinking whisky, listening and trying to imagine what was happening.

At about seven thirty there was a sudden lull, and from down in the square there came a series of small plopping bangs that sounded as if someone were letting

225

off fireworks. A moment or two later, there was a lot of confused shouting from the floor below. I put my glass down and went out on to the terrace. As I did so, there were some more bangs. The Ministry next door was burning and the smoke from it was drifting over to mingle with the stink of shell fumes rising from below. My eyes were smarting anyway. Then, I became aware of another smell and a sudden pain between the eyes. I turned quickly and went back into the room.

"We're going now," I said.

"What is it?"

"Tear gas. If we get too much of it we shan't be able to see to get up to the roof."

As we scrambled through the gap on to the next terrace, our eyes began to stream, but I managed to find the bottle of water and the pistol, and once we were past the rubble we did not have to be so careful about looking where we were going.

I did not have to see now to know what was happening below. The bigger guns were silent, but there was incessant automatic fire and the frame of the building was transmitting an intermittent thudding that was certainly from bursting grenades. There were other sounds, too; the hoarse, inhuman screams and yells that come from men's throats when they are killing at close quarters.

The moment the tear gas had gone in and the

defenders were blinded by it, a party of assault troops in respirators had rushed the Air Terminal. Now, with grenades, machine pistols and *parangs,* they were clearing the ground floor and basements. Other parties would be storming the rear of the building. The business of clearing the upper floors would soon follow. First, more tear gas; then, up the stairs. *"Quick as lightning. Every room. First a grenade, and then yourself. Doesn't matter what's there. Doesn't matter who's there. Then, comb it out with your machine pistol."*

I had already decided where we would go on the roof. There was no cover worth speaking of, and if the defence did last long enough to make a stand there, all we could do would be to lie flat on our faces and hope for the best. The important thing for us was to stay close to the apartment. If Suparto had remembered his promise to warn the assault troops of our presence, we wanted to be there when they arrived. The place I had chosen, therefore, was the section of parapet immediately above the apartment terrace.

We soon found it. The anti-aircraft machine gun which had showered the terrace with cartridge cases had been mounted there, and that part of the roof was strewn with empties. There was a good deal of tear gas about, but most of it seemed to be coming up from below through the ventilators, and when we got to windward of them the air was better. By leaning forward, I could see the terrace below. There was nobody there, and, as far as I could tell, the apartment was still empty. We sat down beside the parapet to dab our eyes and blow our noses and try not to listen to the massacre going on beneath us.

We had been there about twenty minutes when there was a sound of men blundering through the living room immediately below. A moment later Sanusi and Major Dahman came out on to the terrace, coughing and gasping for breath. I could hear others moaning and retching and stumbling about behind them.

It was Dahman who managed to find his voice first.

"Not here, *Boeng*," he said hoarsely.

"Where is Aroff?"

"Aroff is dead, *Boeng*. You saw him."

"Yes. I shall stay here."

"They will take you alive."

"No, they will not do that."

There was a commotion from the passage beyond. A man was shouting something about surrender.

"You are in command, Dahman."

"I will return for you if I can, *Boeng*. But we cannot die like women begging for mercy. We must counter-attack."

He started to cough again as he went back through the living room, but a moment later I heard him gasping out an order about assembling on the stairs. I leaned forward cautiously and looked down on to the terrace.

Sanusi was walking slowly towards the balustrade. He had a machine pistol in his hand. At the end of the terrace he stopped and looked round, drawing deep breaths and wiping his face with the back of his hand. Then, he knelt down and, putting the gun beside him on the ground, began to say his prayers.

He went through the *Rakats;* then, he began to intone a passage from the Koran.

"But what shall teach thee what the night-comer is? It is the star of piercing radiance. Truly every soul has a guardian over it. Let man then reflect out of what he was created. He was created of the poured-forth germs which issue from between the loins and breastbones. Well able truly is Allah, the all-seeing, the all-knowing, the all-merciful, to restore him to life, on the day when all secrets shall be searched out, and he shall have no other might or helper."

I looked down at Rosalie. She took my hand and pressed it against her face.

He was still kneeling there when there was a series of violent explosions that felt as if they were coming from right underneath us, and somewhere not far away a man began screaming. Then, the screaming was drowned by a blast of automatic fire as the assaulting troops reached the head of the staircase.

I saw Sanusi grab the machine pistol, get to his feet and start towards the window. At the same moment a grenade burst in the living room.

229

The blast flung him across the terrace like an empty sack, but he was on his feet in an instant, and as he rose he pressed the trigger of the machine pistol. Someone inside was firing back, and for a few seconds the air was torn to pieces. I saw the grenade land on the terrace outside the bedroom windows just in time to drop behind the parapet. Then, there was an ear-splitting concussion, another burst of automatic fire and silence. When I dared to look down again, three men in steel helmets were walking out slowly on to the terrace.

Two of them looked round warily and then began to move along towards the bathhouse, their arms at the ready. The third man went over to Sanusi's body and shone a flashlight on it. Then, he turned and looked at the bedroom window.

"Mr. Fraser," he called.

"We're up here, Major," I said.

The moon had risen. Down in the square, the dead were still being piled into trucks and driven away, so that, in the morning, when the Minister of Public Enlightenment issued a statement minimising the importance of the whole affair, no sceptical foreign newspapermen would be able to refute his casualty figures. The few surviving wounded were already in sick quarters at the garrison barracks, and therefore inaccessible.

The disabled tank had been hauled on to a transporter and removed. The other tanks had retired together with the self-propelled eighty-eights. The square was being patrolled by two small armoured cars. Now and again there would be a faint rattle of fire from the outskirts of the city as stragglers or would-be escapers were rounded up and killed. The building next door had nearly burned itself out.

There were some eggs left in the kitchen and a Primus stove. While I held the flashlight, Rosalie made an omelette. I salvaged a couple of broken chairs from the chaos in the living room and we ate out on the terrace. It was not comfortable and the smoke still drifted over, but we were very hungry and did not care. We were eating the last of the fruit when Major Suparto returned.

I offered him fruit, but he declined stiffly.

"No, thank you, Mr. Fraser. I have to report to General Ishak and must leave immediately."

"I see. Well, what's the news?"

"I do not think that Miss Linden need feel alarmed for her sister's safety. I am told that there is little damage in that quarter. Apart from that, I regret that the news I have for you is not good. The streets about here are forbidden to civilians at present. If you insist on leaving, I will provide you with an escort, but I do not advise it. The hotels are being searched for rebel sympathisers and many arrests are being made. Emotions have been aroused and matters are a little out of hand. You would be wiser to remain here."

"Oh."

"I can understand your reluctance to stay in this apartment a moment longer than is necessary, but in your own interests it is better that you do."

"Yes. All right."

"There are troops in this building. There is much to be done here. But you will not be disturbed. I have given strict orders. By the morning, perhaps . . ."

"Yes, of course. It's good of you to come and tell us yourself."

He hesitated. It was clear that he was desperately tired, but he also seemed ill at ease, even embarrassed. I wondered why.

"Mr. Fraser," he said, "I may not have the opportunity of seeing you again."

"I'm sorry to hear that."

"You, I think, will soon be leaving Selampang."

"If the police haven't lost my passport in the confusion."

"Should you have difficulties, Lim Mor Sai will arrange matters for you. If you will mention that I suggested that he should."

"Thank you. I was forgetting he was a friend of yours. Will you be going back to Tangga?"

"No. I believe that I am to be given other duties now."

His face had become impassive, and I knew now what was troubling him. He was going to be promoted for his services to the Government, and he had a bad conscience. Aroff's sneer about his treachery had hurt, and I had been there to hear it. He believed that in my heart I despised him. I wished that there were some way of telling him that I did not; and knew that there was no way that would not humiliate us both.

"Gedge will be sorry to hear that," I said; "and so will the Transport Manager."

He smiled sourly. "As Mr. Gedge will shortly be losing his other liaison managers also, perhaps he will feel compensated." The smile went. "And now I regret that I must go."

"Major, I wish that I could begin to thank you . . ."

He broke in hastily. "Please, Mr. Fraser, no thanks. We are both civilised and—what was your word?— *humane* men. Are we not? Yes. I will wish you, as I wished you the other day in Tangga, a safe journey and a happy future."

"Thank you."

He gave Rosalie a curt little bow, and then went back through the living room to the passage door. I followed. As he opened the door, I held out my hand.

"Goodbye, Major."

His handshake was limp; a perfunctory concession to European manners."

"Goodbye, Mr. Fraser."

He went. There was another officer waiting for him in the passage.

I shut the door and bolted it. Then, I walked back through the living room and stood for a moment looking round at the litter and wreckage and filth on the terrace. Where Roda and Sanusi had died there were two large stains, congealed, glistening, and black in the moonlight.

I went over and sat down by Rosalie.

"Do you mind very much that we have to stay here?"

"Now that I am not so worried for my sister, it does not matter."

"Are you still hungry?"

"Not any more."

"Would you like a drink?"

She shook her head. "Do you think that we could have baths?"

"There should be enough water for you."

"For both of us if we use the water carefully. I will show you."

"All right."

So we bathed, pouring the water carefully over one another so that none was wasted, soaping ourselves, and then each rinsing the other. And gradually, as we stood there in the warm darkness, our bodies began to come alive. Nothing was said. We had not touched. We could not see. Yet both of us knew suddenly that it was happening to the other as well. For a moment or two we stood there motionless, each listening to the other's breathing. It became intolerable. I put out my hands and touched her. She drew in her breath sharply; and then her body pressed with desperate urgency against mine.

I picked her up and carried her along the terrace. Somewhere in the wreckage of the bedroom there was a bed. Later, when our bodies had celebrated their return to life and the smell of death had gone, we slept.

10

Soon after eight thirty the next morning I was awakened by someone knocking on the outer door of the apartment. By the time I had found my dressing gown, the knocking had ceased, but there were voices in the passage, one of them a woman's. She sounded annoyed. When I opened the door, Mrs. Choong was waving her door key angrily in the face of a soldier who had come to ask what she was doing there.

She gave a cry of triumph as she saw me. Not only, she said, had she been prevented from coming to work the last two mornings by soldiers in the street, but now, when the soldiers in the street did let her pass, there were other soldiers waiting to accuse her of looting. Her trousers quivered with indignation. When I sent the soldier away she shouted insults after him.

Then, she came in and saw the apartment.

236

For several seconds she stood there staring; then, she waddled through slowly into the living room.

It looked awful in the daylight. The bombing had made a mess, but it had been a tolerable mess; in two days a decorator could have put everything right again. The grenades and machine-pistol fire had savaged the place. The furniture was torn and splintered, the floor and walls and doors were scarred and pitted. Nothing was unspoiled; a pleasant room had become a hideous disfigurement.

To my dismay, I saw tears beginning to roll down Mrs. Choong's plump cheeks.

"Soldiers!" she said bitterly, and then looked at me. "Bedroom also?"

"That's pretty bad, too, I'm afraid, Mrs. Choong."

"Poor Mr. Jebb! But you, mister? You here?"

"Most of the time. Last night, when the attack came, Miss Linden and I went up on the roof."

"Miss Linden? That is Miss Mina's friend?"

"Yes."

"Ah." She brushed the tears away. "You want breakfast?"

"I'm afraid there isn't any food left."

"I bring." She held up the bag she was carrying. "I promise, I bring. Miss Linden, too? She want breakfast?"

"Yes, please, Mrs. Choong. There's no electricity, though. We used the Primus stove."

But she was already in the kitchen. I heard her swearing to herself over the confusion she found there.

After breakfast, Rosalie and I cleaned ourselves up as best we could with the dregs of the water in the bath-house, and made ready to leave. We had arranged to meet later at the Harmony Club. Meanwhile, she would go home and I would see the police about my passport. I would also have to buy some clean clothes. Mrs. Choong took away the dirty ones to get them *dobi*-ed.

Nobody was allowed inside the radio station without a new sort of pass that I did not have, and we had to use the auxiliary staircase to get down into the square. The road was still closed to four-wheeled traffic, but the *betjak* drivers were back, and Mahmud was there, grinning knowingly as if we had all been on a wild two-day party together and were suffering a common hangover. There were a lot of people about, staring awe-struck at the damaged buildings or excitedly discussing their experiences. The children were having a fine time playing in the shell holes. As he pedalled along, Mahmud talked continuously about what had happened where he lived; but I don't think either of us listened to a word he said. We were enjoying our freedom.

When we arrived at Rosalie's apartment house, I waited outside until she had satisfied herself that all was well there, and then went on to the tailor's shop. He had a pair of khaki slacks from another order that

238

he said he could alter for me in an hour, and showed me where I could get a shirt ready-made. After I had bought the shirt, I set out for police headquarters.

As we approached, I could see that there was a big crowd collected at the end of the street in which the headquarters were situated. It soon became apparent that we were not going to be able to get through, and I waited while Mahmud went ahead on foot to see what the trouble was. He was gone five minutes and came back looking troubled. Barbed-wire barricades had been set up at both ends of the street, he said, and troops were preventing anyone entering or leaving who did not have a special pass. The crowd consisted mainly of people with relations who had been arrested during the night. Many of those arrested, he added with gloomy satisfaction, were themselves policemen, but there were others whose only crime was that they had not refused to give food and water to the rebel troops; or so their relatives said.

I went to De Vries' offices, but they were closed. Then, I tried the Orient bar. That was closed, too. As I was coming away, I saw a man I knew slightly who said that there was rumour going around that both the Dutch manager of the Orient and De Vries had been arrested. I went back to the tailor's shop and waited while he finished altering the slacks; then I told Mahmud to take me out to the Harmony Club.

It was a little after eleven and the club did not open until noon, but the doorman was there and he fetched Mrs. Lim.

She was only just sober, and obviously could not remember a thing about me; but she did her best.

"Hullo, love. Fancy seeing you here!"

"Hullo, Mrs. Lim. I'm looking for your husband."

"Oh, he's gone into town. I don't know where. Hasn't it been awful? Where were you all the time? The Orient?"

"Roy Jebb lent me his apartment."

"Dear old Roy. Is he back yet?"

"He should be back today." I could see her memory fumbling dimly with the fact that I knew Jebb.

"And you want to see Mor Sai?"

"That's right. Major Suparto suggested that your husband might be able to advise me about a business matter."

Suparto's name jolted her. She was suddenly wary.

"Major who?"

"Suparto."

"Never heard of him. But Mor Sai'll be here soon. You'd better come in and wait."

"Thanks. While I'm waiting, is there anywhere in the club where I can have a bath and change my clothes?"

"Oh, sure. Charlie there'll show you. I expect you'd like a drink after. I'll see you later in the bar, love."

It was Lim who was waiting for me in the bar when I got there. He nodded politely and we shook hands.

"A drink, Mr. Fraser? Brandy dry?"

"Thanks."

There was no barman there. He went round and poured two, one for himself.

"I hear that you have had a bad time during these troubles, Mr. Fraser."

"Mrs. Lim told you that?" I smiled. "I must have looked rougher than I thought."

"It was not my wife who told me." He pushed a glass across to me and raised his own. "Your health, Mr. Fraser."

"And yours, Mr. Lim."

I took a drink from my glass. He sipped at his, and then put it down and felt in his pocket.

"I think that this is what you wished to see me about," he said, and put my passport on the bar in front of me.

I stared at it uncertainly, then picked it up and looked through the visa pages.

"The exit permit is in order," he said; "and the Customs and exchange clearance papers are clipped to the back."

"This is remarkable, Mr. Lim."

"Oh no. Our friend told me that you had left your passport with the police. I knew that you would not be able to get it, and would come to me. So, to save a journey, I brought it with me."

"You make it sound very simple. I'm deeply grate-ful."

"What have you been able to arrange about your air passage?"

"Nothing. The airline offices are shut. Someone told me that De Vries has been arrested. Is that true?"

"He will be released later, perhaps. But planes can fly without his assistance. Naturally, the scheduled services have been suspended, but foreign airports have been notified now that all is well again. There will be a plane in from Djakarta early this afternoon. It will leave again at five thirty. A passage will, I am certain, be arranged for you."

I smiled. "It sounds as if the Major is in a hurry to get rid of me."

The eyes behind the rimless glasses considered me attentively for a moment. Then, he shrugged. "Why not, Mr. Fraser? You know a little more than is convenient. The longer you are here, the more likely you are to talk to a newspaperman or to a friend who might himself talk."

"I can talk just as well in Djakarta."

"The Major thinks not. He has great confidence in you. Also, he believes that you will not wish to cause difficulties for Miss Linden. No, no, Mr. Fraser. Do not misunderstand. You are not being threatened. Neither is she. It will be no hardship for her to be discreet. We merely ask that you permit her to remain so for the moment. Later, in a week or two, nobody will be interested."

"Well, she'll be here soon. I'll let you know." I paused. "You could have warned me the other night. Why didn't you?"

"I am an agent, not a principal, Mr. Fraser. In such a delicate situation, I was not free to consult my own personal wishes. I was very pleased to hear that you had come to no harm. Another drink?"

"No, thanks."

"Then, if you will excuse me now."

"Of course. And thanks again for the passport."

"If you decide to leave this afternoon . . ."

"Sure, I'll let you know."

Rosalie arrived wearing a dress I had not seen before and looking delightful. She had spoken both to Mina and to her sister. Everything was all right. Mina had not dared to go to the apartment this morning; she had been afraid to find the whole thing blown to pieces and our bodies lying among the ruins. She was going to find a place for Roy to stay while the repairs were being done.

"Poor Roy," I said.

"He will not blame us. We could not help what happened."

"No."

She looked at me quickly. "What is wrong?"

There was nobody else in the bar. I told her about

my passport and the plane that afternoon and what Lim had said. When I had finished, she thought for a moment, then nodded.

"Yes, I see. What is it you wish to do?"

"I want to know what you think. I'm not going to leave here if they're going to make things difficult for you."

"But it is you they are worried about. They know I will say nothing. Isn't that what Lim said?"

"Do you believe him?"

"Oh yes. They know I would not dare."

I knew enough about her now to know when she believed what she was saying; but I persisted.

"Are you sure?"

"Do you not want to go?"

I hesitated. "No, I don't."

"Because of us?"

"Yes."

"I am glad. I, too, had hoped that we could be together again as we were last night. I keep thinking about it. But if they mean you to go, it is better that you go today."

"Yes, I suppose it is."

The barman came in and I ordered some drinks. We drank them and then went in to eat. The food was delicious, but I could not eat very much of it. She scarcely looked at hers. After a bit I gave up trying.

"Rosalie."

Her eyes met mine. She said softly: "Yes, it is the same with me. I cannot stop thinking. What time must you be at the airport?"

"Five, I should think."

"If you went back to the Air House and packed your things, we could be together until it is time for you to go."

"Where?"

"At my home. My sister will not be there. It is very small and not like Roy's apartment, but you will not mind that."

"No, I won't mind."

As soon as we were ready to leave, I went into the bar and found Lim.

"About that air passage. What do I do about the ticket?"

"It is at the airport reception office, waiting for you, Mr. Fraser."

"You were pretty sure of me, weren't you?"

"Not of you, Mr. Fraser. But I was sure of Miss Linden. She is an honest and clear-thinking person. Do you not agree?"

Back at the apartment, I found that Jebb had returned and was surveying the damage with Mrs. Choong.

"Well, Roy," I said.

"Well, chum," he answered grimly; "I bet that's the last time you mind anybody's place for them."

"I'm sorry, Roy. But first the bombing and then the grenades and stuff. There was nothing we could do. You see . . ."

"I'm not blaming you, you silly bastard, I'm apologising! How do you think I felt in Makassar, sitting there listening to the bloody radio and wondering how you were getting on up here? I'd sooner have been here myself. I was afraid I'd killed you, dammit! Where were you when all this happened?"

I told him a bit about it. He listened and swore at intervals, and then asked after Rosalie.

"She's fine. I'm going to see her in a minute. I'm leaving today."

"My word! On that five-thirty plane?"

"That's right."

"Who fixed that? People are fighting to get on it."

"Lim Mor Sai."

"What did I tell you? He can fix anything. Well, I'll see you out at the airport. I've got to go out there to clear some stuff through Customs. I came straight in as soon as I touched down. Seen anything of Mina?"

"No, but she's trying to find somewhere for you to live while this is being repaired."

"That means a camp bed in her place. See you later, Steve."

When he had gone, I packed. It did not take long. Mrs. Choong fetched my things from the *dobi* laundry. They were still damp. But I stuffed them into my suitcase anyway. Then I gave Mrs. Choong a present and went downstairs again for the last time.

I had told Mahmud to wait for me and he was there at the door. On the way, I stopped at a shop in the Chinese quarter and bought a silver box with an amethyst set in the lid. When I had paid for it, I took out all the money I had left on me, set aside what I would need to pay Mahmud, buy my ticket to Djakarta and bribe the Customs at the airport, and put the rest in the box. Then I went on to see Rosalie.

There were two rooms, one hers, one her sister's. They were clean and simple, like rooms in a kampong house, with bamboo blinds on the windows and mosquito nets over the beds. There was a small verandah with orchids growing in pieces of tree bark.

When it was time for me to go, I went over to the bed and looked down at her. She was lying there with her eyes closed and her body shiny with sweat. There was a smile on her lips. I thought that she might be asleep.

I put the box down on the small table as quietly as I could, but she heard and opened her eyes. For a moment she looked up at me; then her eyes went to the table and she sat up quickly.

"No."

"You said that if we had liked one another it would make the parting easier."

"That was before."

"For me it needs to be made easier."

"And for me."

"Then this is the best way. Open it later when I've gone."

I bent over and kissed her once more.

"We love each other," she said.

"Yes."

"But we are also wise."

"I believe so."

"Yes." She smiled. "This way we shall always remember each other with love."

A few moments later I carried my suitcase down the long, steep staircase and walked out into the blinding sun.

Mahmud had put the hood up, and I sat in the shade of it trying to think of the journey ahead as he pedalled me out to the airport.